Richard Carpenter's

ROBIN OF SHERWOOD

SANCTUARY

by Paul Birch

Originally published in 2019 by
Chinbeard Books & Spiteful Puppet
in partnership with the
Richard Carpenter Estate
The edition published in 2021
www.spitefulpuppet.com

Layout & adaptation for this edition by
Andrews UK Limited
www.andrewsuk.com

SANCTUARY

It started with an arrow

It sank into the flank of the roe causing her to twist back on herself mid-run. An acrobatic flip in the freezing air before she found herself falling on frozen ground, warming the snow with blood, melting it with her dying breaths. In her last moments she heard the sounds of hard hooves and caught the scent of unfamiliar men on expensive horses of war.

Those same horses stumbled on the root ridden track. They were bred for the battlefield and not the uneven paths of the King's forest. Before they rode, the armoured men had swapped their helmets for hoods – for only a fool would wear armour when you needed to see more than an inch in front of your face. But now the flakes were falling thick and sticky as mud and so their bitter mouths were cursing against winter's kiss. It was not hard to track a wounded deer in the snow and yet they had lost her. The dogs weren't with them, too sensible to leave a warm kennel even when sticks were employed, and so a scent would not be picked up.

The men could not see their quarry. They could not see the kind hands of the hooded man who gently calmed the roe in her last moments. Firm hands, a prayer and the granting of a quick mercy to end the suffering, Robin of Loxley pulled out the arrow. The swallowtail head was well crafted and with a steel tip: not the work of a cheap smithy. These men were far from home and they were making too much bawdy noise to be serious about the hunt. The men were drunk to keep out winter's chill; but not even a cask of honey wine could help with being snow-blind. They had blood on their hands but held no real concern about taking their trophy home. A poacher would lose his life for loosing an arrow at the King's deer whether it hit or not. These men, it seemed, could shoot for pleasure and go unpunished. They showed more interest in killing the hours than in the creature that now lay dead in Sherwood. The spilling of blood was nothing new to them.

The Sheriff was on his prize palfrey. She was fast, expensive and bore an astonishing resemblance to a remarkably thin bishop he once had known. The likeness really was extraordinary but what, he had decided, he liked most about the horse was that it made him look rather dashing. Almost regal. It wasn't that it simply gave him some much needed height but that the horse's proportions helped create the illusion that he, himself, could be somewhat heroic. That illusion was now very much being destroyed by riding with these reprobates. One of the men, John Salveyn, was using his baselard to act out an obscene story concerning a knight and a miller's daughter; the climax of which caused him to fall from his horse, much to the delight of the other men. The Sheriff found himself rolling his eyes. He knew it was cliché but he felt the need to make some silent protest about the company he was forced to keep in these days before Christmas. The Knights Bachelor were doing the rounds; moving from castle to castle in the hope of finding work or at least some sport. They were landless mongrels too low on the courtly ladder to have an estate but far too high to have any real employment. It was either Knight or Priest and these men were not cut out for Holy Orders.

No one dared call them mercenaries, not when they had been anointed by the King's sword, but it was what they were and, of course, you could always show a mercenary the door. Gilbert De Grant or Stephen of Wallingford, however, were Nobles and needed to be welcomed with open arms. After their notorious exploits in Leicester had run their unfortunate course it was now Nottingham's turn. This energetic band of roister-doisters had presented themselves, late one night, at the castle. Gisburne, that bone-headed numbskull, was delighted for they seemed to be cut from the same cloth. Cock fighting, bear baiting and a quick game of 'hard-knuckle harry' seemed to now have replaced honest conversation. Violence as sport, that peculiar English disease, seemed to be spreading under the banner of the Knights Bachelor. A celebration of cruelty. It would become increasingly hard, the Sheriff had pondered, to use violence as a severe tool for maintaining order when these ruffians were dispensing it as freely as water. Butchery was losing its currency. In truth, he sincerely hoped they would grow tired and the festering fools depart before Christmas so he could eat his goose in peace. On the other hand, a man who wished to rise, will always have need of such men and so, reluctantly, he found himself on a freezing morning riding uncomfortably through treacherous snow with Gisburne's new playmates and attempting to indulge them before they decided to move on to pastures new. He had even shot a deer by accident. Considerably bored he had fired into the woods and ended hitting a creature he didn't even know was there. There was rejoicing as the animal screamed. This, at least, should have brought the miserable endeavour to a quick end but now the fools couldn't even find the thing. Instead, the men were shouting. Piers Swynbourne had drawn his sword whilst Gilbert was excitedly pointing to the forest as if he had never seen a tree before. The Sheriff followed the knight's gaze expecting to finally see his unintended trophy and instead saw something else. *Someone* else. Yes. Robert de Rainault, the Sheriff of Nottingham saw the outlaw standing there; and the outlaw had blood on his hands.

Robin caught the Sheriff's gaze and cursed himself for his stupidity. For wanting to see the faces of the men who had killed the deer. Now he had been seen. Now, he was the one who would be hunted. He hurled himself back towards the heart of the forest and away from the wide paths of the woodland's outskirts and the Sheriff's men. He could not run apace for the snow craftily covered root, hole, bush and track as if they all were the same. A misplaced step could lead to a sprained ankle which would, no doubt, result in a broken neck courtesy of the hangman. Nevertheless, he guessed and hopped and twisted to find firm forest path; helping put some distance between himself and the horses who would find the chase even more difficult. His boots were sodden, though, and the cold slowed his joints. What had happened? A fierce winter always kept the war between Nottingham and Sherwood at bay with both sides showing more concern with staying warm than in firing up new feuds. Merchant traffic largely ceased and everyone relied on their stockpiled food and wood to keep them through the dark days of wintertide. It had long been Robin's fear that the Sheriff would take advantage of the cruelties of the season – when the outlaws were weakened through lack of food and warmth – and send a small army into the forest. Now it seemed that was exactly what was happening.

The horns were sounding as if it were Judgement Day. The beginning of the end. Robin turned back to look at the men in pursuit. Again, he cursed himself for his folly. Looking back was something he was constantly telling his band never to do as it would only ever slow them down. A wrong look had got him into this and another could cost him his life. This time, however, the look saved it. A panicked turn was enough to put space between him and the crossbow bolt that now splintered the ash tree directly in front. The shot wavered the snow in his path. A crossbow? The weapon of a soldier not a hunter. Did they have any idea what they were doing? Was this an accident or had they been coming for him all along? He ran now for it was too late for anything but bold and reckless risk. To his left, part sprint, part skid, with no idea where he was going. This was not his usual territory and he was far from the heart of Sherwood; far from anywhere he might have expected to run in to this kind of trouble. He had come all the way to the east, almost to Marten Moor; forced by the snows to forage further and farther to find food. He did not know these paths and they were making a mockery of his flight. More than once he slipped and his hunters gained ground. The horses were not fast but they were big and strong and would sooner trample a new, more direct path, than follow an old one.

Left again, under branch and stumbling through black thorn – the hidden spikes puncturing his legs, slowing him once more. The pursuing horses were quieter now. A bad sign: the beasts concentrating on unfamiliar ground and gaining confidence with every second. The crack of another crossbow bolt and the noise of men were louder. They could see him and were firing. He was within their grasp. Robin made another left through thickly covered branches of Wych Elm and Juniper and found himself running blind, like a fool, out of the forest.

Out into the open.

He hadn't intended it but the horsemen had forced him back out of the forest. An impossible position. Exposed. If the Knights made their way out onto this plain he would be easily cut down. Blood pounded in his ears as he tried to think. Sherwood and its sanctuary was at his back. There was nothing but field for the plough to his left and right – and frozen fields were not going to save him. His only chance lay before him: the frozen river Idle and beyond it the only building in sight, a poor man's church.

Its roof covered by a murder of dark black crows, the ominous place was built with rough stone to last the ages but blackened by fire at its base, as if some hate filled mob had tried to remove it from the earth. And why not? It was a malformed thing, crudely made by untrained hands and it was awkwardly set. Built in the fork of a river on sodden earth as if someone had determined a monument of hope should be constructed in one of misery. But it was hope and so he began to run towards it. There was no bridge but surely the ice would hold him..?

The Sheriff was the first to see him. He had had no intention of riding his expensive horse into a frozen forest and so, instead, let Gisburne's bastards lead the hunt into the greenwood whilst he urged his horse to skirt the edge of the tree-line following, as best he could, the glorious noise of men who love nothing better than to chase and kill other men. It was an easy task for they did so like the sound of their own voices. They were still stuck within the forest when it happened. The wolfshead had stumbled out of the trees and was running for the church. If you could call it running. He seemed hampered by the cold and appeared to be slightly wounded. The Sheriff was reminded of a hapless rabbit who, in the chaos of the chase, runs hither and yon, despite knowing that it will soon be in a pot. A frantic last effort before the inevitable finish.

He breathed out. It had been a long time since he had directly killed a man – after all that was what you had a Gisburne for – but his baser nature assured him he would probably enjoy killing this one. He didn't fancy his chances with a bow, even at this range but that fine horse of his could certainly run a man down. He spurred his horse on and on. Iron on the hooves pounding hard into frozen earth. His heart was beating fast and, for a moment, he began to get excited. Perhaps the Knights Bachelor had a point. Perhaps that merry havoc which so delighted them was beginning to stir in his own veins. The wind was behind him as if Herne had sent him a boon.

Robin heard the horse and knew this time he could not afford to look behind. He knew he could not outrun the animal and it was a simple matter of seconds before the beast would be upon him. He continued to try and run with his feet pressing on through snow, finally landing on the ice which held. But the snow was thick and the slippery surface slowed him again. If he could make it to the church, bar the doors – it would give him a little time. But he didn't *have* time. The Sheriff's horse was almost on him. He darted right only to find himself falling flat onto his stomach. His head hit the ice and his nose was bloodied. The river had betrayed him. It was surely over. He turned onto his back only to realise the horse was not on him. He pulled himself to his sodden feet only to see that the animal had slowed to a curious trot when its hooves left land for frozen waste. The Sheriff kicked and cursed and the horse began to canter. It was not fast but it was gaining, and and he could already hear the Sheriff's laugh carried on the icy wind.

That was when the screaming started. From the bell tower. A poor priest was looking down on them. He was shouting so furiously it was impossible to tell if he was yelling for mercy or urging the sheriff on with his bloody business. The crows flew from the roof as if scattered by magic; just before the man started ringing the cracked bell. The noise alarmed the world, breaking the wintery silence with a discordant peal. Broken. Tuneless. It was a mockery of sound which, at least, had the virtue of drowning out Robert de Rainault's triumphant cackle. The knights would soon come. The Sheriff made the mistake of looking back to see if the Knights Bachelor and Gisburne would be witness to the Sheriff's killing of the notorious Robin in the Hood. A mistake. It's always a mistake to look back and Robin took his chance. A distracted Sheriff grinning back at the forest was not looking at his prey.

He was not looking when the object of the hunt became the hunter and ran towards his pursuer. Robin cast his bow and arrows aside – throwing them to the bank. His feet did not slip, each stride finding resolute ground as if Herne himself had charmed his path. He ran. He leapt, and as the bell rang out its dissonant song, he tackled the Sheriff from his horse and they fell together.

The priest watched from on high. And he tolled the bell as if summoning judgement upon them all. He watched with sadness as one man of blood leapt upon another and so he rang in sorrow. Each toll sending out a sharp warning to the world, loud and brash enough to break the ice. The bell rung out once, twice, thrice, and more as a horse toppled and the hunter and hunted fell. The ice finally cracked and they fell further still; the newly revealed river swallowing them whole.

They called her by many names: Nan of the waters, Jenny Greenteeth, Waterwitch, Maid o' the weeds... Robin recalled them all. There were many who knew, all too well, the pain she could inflict when, with watery arms, she would snatch a child or a drunken husband fool enough to walk too close to the river. When the mood took her she would drag them down to her bed and keep them there until her long loneliness was eased.

It was a story, of course, for although there are many strange things that haunt the earth in shadow and in twilight – a river monster is not one of them. She was a figure, from a cautionary tale, told to keep the community safe. To remind them that a river, whilst it brings life, can also bring death.

Now, Robin was being brought to death. The icy waters filled his ears with a bubbling lullaby; shut his eyes with a freezing dark; washed the blood from his nose and hushed his senses with its calming embrace. He was alone as the current pulled him under. The Sheriff had been swept away from under him and, although they had all fallen into the waters as a couple, the river had pulled them apart. If they were to drown it would not be together. The panic had also been washed away. Just as the clothes are taken from a dead man before burial so Robin stripped was of his fears of the day: the pursuit in the forest, the chase over the ice, the desperate underwater clawing to find a way back to the surface all had given way to a hypnotic peaceful stillness.

All he had to do was float.

Robin dreamed... or perhaps it was a memory of a dream that Herne had once shared with him? He could not tell, for time, like breath, was nowhere to be found. Hope, regret, past, present and future were all simply driftwood. He was neither here nor there and yet he must be somewhere for he found himself now facing Herne. The figure swam towards him from waters made of light but here he was in a different form. Here was Herne, not the Hunter but the Fisherman, green with weeds, a willowy creature swimming in the waters. No, *was* the waters. Robin tried to speak and found his words mere bubbles; as if nothing he said was of any consequence. He could hear a bell now. Ringing in his ears but this bell was beautiful. Resonant. Harmonious. A song was being sung and sung so beautifully it began to warm his body. The bell that was also a song also became words in his mind. Herne's words or perhaps his? It was impossible now to tell where one thing started and another began. Was this a revelation or something he had always known? Was this lunacy or prophecy? The words were as clear to him as the water:

In the Season of the Christ Child the Eel and the Wolf and the Hawk did dance a furious jig; and where one finished and the other began... no man could tell. And in that dance there was a kiss and a death and a saving but who did what to whom... no man could tell.

They were faint but clear. His heart began to beat. He hadn't realised it had stopped but as the words were spoken as melody so his heart began to mark time again. A drum. An underscore to the refrain that repeated itself, louder now, loud enough for the words to become chaotic pictures. His heart was drumming louder too and he watched the creatures move and tangle and embrace each other. It was slow at first and then faster and faster.

His heart was now beating so fast and loud he could barely hear the words only watch the creatures circle and weave and embrace. There was a harmony in it but it was a strange harmony. Unsettling. His heart was beating but not in time and with every beat it felt as if it might burst from his chest. He found his body dancing, kicking, moving, swimming; a frantic dance to the strangest song he had ever heard:

And in that dance there was a kiss and a death and a saving but who did what to whom... no man could tell.

A prophecy? A memory? A dream?

Or the nonsense of man slowly drowning in an ice cold river.

The man kicked and thrashed like a newborn as the priest pulled him from the waters. A reverse baptism. This strange infant was strong and his muscular body made heavier by the river's pull. It took effort, the priest observed, to save the wretch but what was salvation without cost? He gripped the man's waterlogged tunic with an iron grip. His hands had cut stones from a quarry, taken iron from fire, had rebuilt a church and so it was with a determined and practiced strength that he pulled the dark-haired stranger onto the river bank.

The thrashing stopped as the man coughed up water into the snow. The priest had seen this kind of thing before and he knew to turn the fellow onto his side. Sometimes what came out was river water, sometimes sick, but what he recalled seeing most was the vomiting of blood. He had seen that most in the desert. That was where he had first learned to turn a man in the hope of saving a life. There was no blood this time, however, and, once the water had finished running its course, he heard the man begin to breathe. Sleep would no doubt come next but sleep could sometimes be as dangerous as the water the man had just rejected.

The priest flipped the saturated body over his shoulder as easily as a sack of grain. He was an enormous man and it made him melancholy to think that so many people often found such a shepherd so intimidating. He supposed that some shepherds were made to tend to their flock whilst men like himself were built to keep the wolves at bay. Besides, being strong had its advantages. If he wasn't he would not, perhaps, have been the one up on the roof repairing the bell tower and who would have seen them fall then? He had tried to warn them. Tried to shout to the strangers that they were on the ice but they were too concerned with attacking each other to hear his words. Their sins luring them to their own mutual destruction. That was when he rang the bell which seemed to have distracted them for a moment before their bloodlust overcame their reason and the waters took them. He might be large but the priest was also nimble and it was not long before he was at the river's edge.

Once again he opened the door to the church. The oak door was heavy and reluctant to move and so the priest had to use real force to open it with one heavy arm whilst carrying the man securely with the other. Once inside he laid the fellow down. Could he save him? It was not certain. He had learned a little medicine, here and there, and he hoped his prayers were powerful. There were many that he had lost; and that troubled him for men were not always fit for heaven when they left this world. He would do his best. He was, it was true, a poor sort of shepherd, but then, looking at the drenched body on the floor, this was a poor sort of lamb. The creature's breath began to fade and so the priest began to work.

Robin's eyelids were heavy with fatigue but he forced himself to open them. He expected to see the familiar rock roof of the secret winter cave that the outlaws resided in when the snows came. The view was altogether different; instead he found himself looking at the vast roof of a broken down church. His thoughts swam and for one brief moment he feared he was imprisoned in Nottingham castle. He tried to move but found his body weak and unresponsive. He felt a hard table underneath his back which was constantly being moved. Some fool was rattling it; trying to shake him off. No. He was the one shaking. Shivering, despite a heavy woollen blanket placed across his chest and arms. He tried to raise his neck and, from his prone position, could just about see his bare feet. It looked like the blanket had been pulled up to expose his legs. Was he naked? Where was his sword? Albion was gone! How could he have let what was entrusted to him so easily be taken?

He moved a feeble arm underneath his scratchy bedcover and realised his clothes were gone too, replaced with a dark woollen tunic. It reminded him of Tuck's impossibly large garment – better suited to the slow conduct of the friary than the fast living of the forest. It always amazed him that Tuck never seemed to trip or get tangled in the briars and branches of Sherwood. Was Tuck here?

It was then he remembered. They had all woken, that morning, in the dark of the cave. There were many in Wickham that believed Robin's men to sleep out under the stars every night or else in leafy pine shelters as if they were immune to the rain, the snow, the frost and the cold. In the dark months of the year there were many times when all wondered if they could survive. Robin himself feared winter more than the wrath of Nottingham.

Herne had showed him the place they could live in these times. A network of small caves older even than the ancient forest itself. An old place. An ancient place. Part of the river trickled through a channel in the south wall and so there was always water and Herne's charms seemed to keep the place from being besieged by rats and mould. It was in this place they stored and dried out logs throughout the year. It was, in many ways, a fortress against nature.

'If this place ever fell we'd all be in the grave,' Will Scarlet had grumbled once.

They kept grain here, nuts and seeds along with dried out meats to sustain the long hungry hours when hunting and fishing became impossible. Marion, always the shrewdest, allocated the duties of the day. Today Much was supposed to travel east to the forest but he had been downcast of late and so Marion suggested he work on building up the stock of arrows. He was tasked with crafting the heads on a makeshift forge in the belly of the cave. It was hot and smoky work but, at least, the fire might warm his body if not his spirits. It fell to Robin, then, to track and hunt. He was the better shot and the mood of the company lifted when he agreed to the task. He had been hunting for the past week, often coming back empty handed, but, of all the men, he had also brought home the most food. Where were his friends now? Looking for him? What would they do when he did not return? He had been careful to cover his initial tracks but it wouldn't take an experienced woodsman to simply head east and find the devastating trail left by the knights and their horses. The very thought of them made blood rush through his veins and he forced himself to sit up. Perhaps a more significant question would be to ask how long before those same knights found their way to this church?

Then he saw his legs. They were so blue they seemed to belong to another creature entirely. He could not move his toes and he feared the frost might have claimed them. There was an array of cuts and slashes from his flight through the forest. How cruel nature was to take away the fruit in winter but leave the thorn.

It was then that a giant of man came at him with a knife.

Robin saw the figure, who must have been near all this time, come out of the shadows almost as if he were made of shadows himself. The blade was red; not with blood but reflecting a fire which must be burning nearby. Robin immediately try to roll from the makeshift table but found a large hand, almost the span of his own head, placed upon his shoulder and pushing him back down on his back.

'Steady,' said the giant, as if he were talking to a horse. 'Steady now.'

Robin fell back onto the table; his bones falling as easily as skittles in an ale house. The knife rose and fell and presently a bandage came into view. The man put the knife aside, and, having cleaned a particularly deep wound by Robin's knee, he began to wrap the leg. He was big. Very big. This explained the size of the robe in which Robin found himself. The pain began to subside a little. It was strange but, in his fever, he had not even noticed it was there until, thanks to the work of the giant, it began to fade.

'Who..?' began Robin, but, at the very moment, his eyes betrayed him and everything became dark.

He woke again to the find the hands of the man dressing the wounds on his legs. Although he was large he tended to his work with a practiced care. He held a shorter knife now. Both handle and blade were curved and, for a brief moment, it looked like he was holding a snake. Nearby was a barrel, rolled into the centre of the church and used as a side table. The remnants of cut herbs: betony and comfrey, long past their summer freshness, littered both blade and barrel top. He felt the pain now, his wounds making an angry complaint. And he ached. His whole body felt like he had been beaten by quarterstaff and cudgel. Had he been beaten or had a sickness claimed him? His lungs hurt as if he had ran through a fire and swallowed its burning smoke.

He remembered the river then. Remembered his run at the Sheriff, his foolhardy leap and the perilous fall into the water as the ice beneath them had shattered. Was the Sheriff dead? If so, it was an invisible act, for the knights had been fighting their way out of the forest when he threw himself at the horse. Perhaps the consequences of such an act would not be blamed on the outlaws? If they were who knows what fury the King might bring to Nottingham? The people would pay dearly and that, surely, was his fault. If, however, it was seen as an act of God or a drunken mistake when the Sheriff was found floating in the River Idle then perhaps there would be no wrath? The king might even appoint a more just commissioner and he might be free to lead a peaceful life.

No.

There was the bell. The dreadful noise of that fateful bell and the priest who had rung it. He had seen what happened. How could he have missed it, perched, as he was, with the malevolent crows on that roof? A ruthless man might need to stop the mouth of that priest. Might need to cause his breath to cease. It would be an evil act but how could sparing the common people untold and unnumbered future miseries be unjust? Perhaps he could simply ask the priest for his silence? Even if the Sheriff was still alive the assault had been in plain sight. A man of the church would never go against God by going against the King. Never. Tuck had, of course, but this man, apart from being a cleric, did not seem to have the same light spirit. If anything, the single witness to the attack on the Sheriff of Nottingham, who was now redressing

11

the wounds on his legs, seemed deeply troubled and troubled thoughts tended to fall out of unhappy mouths. A bargain would be out of the question. The priest who had saved his life was now also its biggest threat. It wasn't usual for him to have these dark thoughts but perhaps that time in the water had changed him?

A brazier filled with logs was near warming them both and drying Robin's clothes. Its flames cast shadows of the priest on the walls; menacing reflections of the man who now held Robin's life in his hands. Robin slowly sat up. It was a little easier this time. He couldn't stay here and it was not just the danger of a loose tongued priest that might get him killed.

'We must b-b-bar the doors,' said Robin attempting to manoeuvre himself from the table.

The Priest's giant hand, once again, firmly held him on the makeshift table that had been set up in the nave. He nodded towards the porch and Robin looked and was relieved to see an oak beam barring the doors.

'I don't think we will be easily interrupted,' said the priest.

Robin relaxed a little and, for the first time, got a clear look at the kind and benevolent face staring back at him. It was worn. Time had carved out many lines and callouses on his visage. He did not look like the smooth pale clerics who haunted Nottingham with purple robes and golden rings. Those men floated in their finery above the world so that mud would never so much as touch their shoes. Riches. Power. These men knew nothing of earthly matters and, he suspected, even less of heavenly ones. All they knew was comfort and pleasure. This priest was different. He looked as if suffering had been carved into his face by life's stonemason. Perhaps that was where his compassion came from? He felt safe; or at least for the moment. Robin smiled in gratitude. The priest smiled back. A broad smile with lips peeled back. That was when Robin's heart began beating in alarm because when the priest grinned you could see all his teeth. This smiling saviour revealed every single tooth and they were all there – perfect, unbroken and… entirely black.

'You're shivering,' said the priest, pulling another thick blanket from a pile on the floor. 'Your wounds are dressed so you can wrap tight in this. The cloth will not infect you. A man pulled from the river needs to keep his blood hot.'

'You s-s-saved me,' Robin stuttered, trying to speak more clearly, though his jaw was still trembling from the cold. He almost wished he were asleep again.

The priest saw him shivering and took an iron to move the logs in the brazier. They hissed in protest at his interference but this small act of violence made the fire burn hotter. 'You're not saved yet. Their arrows, their swords and their horses didn't kill you. But more men have died from the river than from weapons of war. I pulled you from the waters but the waters could still claim you. It gets in your bones.'

'I can feel it.' replied Robin.

'Better that you do feel the chill. It's when you can't feel *anything* you need to fear. Pain is sometime's God's way of letting you know you're still alive. Pleasure is the road to death, no? She lured you to her bed and you followed like most men do.'

Robin was unclear as to what the priest was referring too. Was he talking about Marion? Did the churchman know who he had in his care and, if so, how much it would be worth his while to hand him over to Gisburne and his ilk.

'The river is a jealous whore,' continued the priest, 'she freely embraces but she does not like to let go. Get warm, Loxley. Christmas is coming and we have work to do.'

Loxley? So, he did know. Was this why he was going to all this trouble? He was clearly worth more alive than dead. Was this the work of charity or that of a mercenary?

The fire crackled and its unstable blaze kept recasting the present drama in entirely different lights. As the priest prepared what appeared to be some kind of liniment, the fire would illuminate the man and reveal a monstrous looking figure; red, scarred and entirely suited to a hellish battlefield. Then there would be a mysterious crackle, and the fire would shift and its light reveal, instead, a gentle man of God busy with the business of healing. It must be his imagination playing tricks or perhaps it was a fever? Whatever the reason it was making Robin feel profoundly unsettled.

Robin wrapped himself in the blanket. It was heavy and thick like those a crusader might take to Nasir's lands, of which, in the cold of those caves Nasir would talk of their heat and that the nights could be bitter than the coldest of English winters. It was hard to believe coming from a man so evidently kissed by the sun but there was not a soul among them who accounted Nasir to be a liar. Thinking about the men hurt almost as much as the pain in his legs. Where were they? Safe? Were they even now fighting those well-equipped knights or were they all dead? Was that why no-one had come to the church?

His body was wracked with the exhaustion of the day and his tormented thoughts. The comforting weight of the blanket soon proved impossible to resist. He wanted to get up, find his clothes and escape back to the safety of the greenwood; but there was little fight left and soon he was lost, once again, in a slumbering darkness.

His nose woke him this time. The scent of a rich hot broth working its way to directly to his stomach. Food? He couldn't remember the last time he had eaten anything other than seeds and acorn mulch. Immediately he felt stronger. The pains of his chase began to make themselves known again; but he was warm and found he could speak without stammering like a fool.

'How long have I been asleep?'

'Long enough,' said the priest handing him a bowl of nourishing soup. 'The day grows old. Eat.'

'They haven't come... the knights? Your bell... they must have heard.'

'True enough. But when the idle floods it turns this useless patch of land on which the church stands into an island. There is no boat. There is no bridge save the ice and, as you found, only a fool would tread there. We are alone.' The priest began to tuck into his own bowl. He ate quickly as if there were no time left in the world. Robin, wondered, if they were so alone what would cause a man to consume his meal as if the devil were on his back.

'They could risk the ice.'

'They could and then they would find themselves also in my care or in the care of the riverbed. Perhaps they have more sense than an outlaw and a Sheriff.'

Sheriff. So he knew that too. All was lost. He had been seen attacking the Sheriff. There could be no deception. Perhaps it was appropriate for the truth of this dreadful day to be laid bare in a church.

The priest looked squarely at him. 'Eat. My prayers alone won't save you '

Robin drank the soup. It was bitter and losing its warmth quickly. 'I thank you for your kindness but I would be safer in Sherwood. If the knights are not outside—'

'They are not,' interrupted the priest.

'Then, I will return to the forest.'

'Return to your folly, you mean. '*Sicut canis qui revertitur ad vomitum.*'

'I don't understand.'

'As a dog returns to its own vomit so fools repeat their folly.' I know you, Loxley. You are the outlaw. The thief. The robber. The devil worshipper who prostitutes himself for the stag.' replied the priest. It was not said in anger but, simply, and without the tone of judgement. He said it in the same way he had offered Robin a blanket. The tone was soft but the words were harsh and there was something about those dark black teeth that made Robin feel a spell was being cast; although he was not sure which of them was under enchantment.

'I am trying to save our people.' Robin used the word 'our' deliberately. This was not the first time he found himself at the mercy of an uncertain host and he knew he had to rely on the cleric's assistance. At least for now.

'And yet you cannot even save yourself. The Lord has struck you down, Loxley.'

'It was an accident.'

'Driven by bloodlust. A saint would have floated across that river. He would have been upheld. You don't believe me because you are not a believer and that is to be expected. But, I am telling you, the ice broke under the weight of your iniquities. Yet, He is merciful and has used my hands to raise you up. Take comfort from that. It is clear to me that you are here for a purpose.'

Robin was struck by the lack of guile. The priest truly believed in everything he said and that, in these times, was rare. The question was what purpose did the man have in mind? Could it be a reward and money for the church or was this the beginning of a new ally in helping bring justice for the people? Could this giant of a man be a new and holy warrior of Sherwood? He would be useful, of that there could be no doubt. Robin leaned forward, 'You said that "we have work to do?" '

'Yes. It will be hard… and so you must recover your strength.'

'I've eaten.'

'I can see.'

'And I would recover quicker under greenwood in the care of my friends. Let me go and I'll return and give you whatever assistance you require as soon as I am strong. You will see that I am not the evil man you think I am. I keep my word.'

The priest tilted his head and looked benignly at Robin as if he were a child. 'In the summer months the river is filled with eels. They come and I set my basket in the waters just after I ring the bell for Prime. The day begins and, when it ends, I take my basket and they are filled with them. You see how the Lord provides? Then I take a tenth of the eels and throw them back in the water; for this is my gift back to God. Then, I take another tenth for myself, for this is His gift to me. The rest I give to the poor. This is the way of heaven.'

Once again, Robin struggled to understand the parable. Why did clerics enjoy talking in riddles? The one thing that seemed clear was that both men, different though they were in stature and station, were trying to make a difference to the common man. 'You are generous,' said Robin appealing to the priest's sense of charity. 'We also help the poor for –

The priest cut him off with a sharp look, leaning in close. Robin couldn't remember a more terrifying face. His eyes were not unkind but his breath had the stink of disease about it.

The priest began to whisper, 'My brother, the time has not yet come for you to speak this way. If you have ears to hear then listen to what I am telling you. I take my eels and they know not what is to come. They twist and turn and slip and slide – so very desperate to return to their home – to return to the river whore. We mustn't judge them. It is what they know. It is where they feel safe. But they are predestined for my plate. It is what they were created for. And, so I take my knife and cut their heads off and, in this way, they are no longer troubled or anxious about returning home. So too, a man will never have peace until he fulfils God's purpose.

'If they catch me neither of us will fulfil "God's purpose," responded Robin. 'The Sheriff and his men will return with boats, or a makeshift bridge and they will take us both. Even burn this church to the ground! Please… give me my clothes before your 'kindness' kills us both.'

The priest looked at Robin with surprise and then he began to laugh. It echoed around the church as if it were a hymn of praise. 'Is that what you are worried about, little eel? You don't understand do you? It's impossible for the Sheriff to come here.'

Impossible. So, it was true. The battle between them was over. Robin, felt strangely upset. 'The Sheriff…' he began, 'the Sheriff is dead?'

The priest laughed again. 'No. Of course not.'

'But you said it was "impossible for him to come here". How do you know he won't return?'

'Because,' smiled the priest. 'He's already here. He was the wretch I pulled out first.'

Robin's legs were weak but the priest was strong. The large cleric had his arm around Robin's waist was helping him move slowly through the church. The building was not big but, once they had moved from the immediacy of the fire and into the shadows, there was a peculiar darkness which made the space hard to fathom. His vision began to play tricks and, on more than one occasion, he thought he saw something move in the blackness; yet none of these phantoms ever seem to strike. His eyes might be deceiving him but his ears remained keen and he heard Robert de Rainault's muffled voice long before he came into view.

There was a bundle of protesting rags tied to a pillar in the south transept. As the priest led a limping Robin closer it was clear that wrapped in ragged blankets, as if he were a beggar's Christmas present, was the keeper of the King's Peace; the furious Sheriff of Nottingham. He was bound at the legs, tied across the chest to a stone pillar, and gagged at the mouth.

Robin silently wondered why he had not been afforded the same treatment. The priest, as if reading his mind, said, 'My Lord Sheriff did not pay heed. I warned him that the time had not yet come for him to speak but he was insistent. Had he continued his voice would have stopped me from my work and you from your recovery. Do not be concerned for he has not been harmed.'

This seemed to be the case and, as he surveilled the captive Sheriff, he realised his own sight was beginning to adjust to the light in this part of the sanctuary. The ragged officer seemed perfectly well and the only obvious wound was to his dignity. As they came closer the Sheriff began to utter threats from behind his gag. The words were lost but the tone was unmistakably clear.

The priest gently lowered Robin to the ground next to a pillar opposite the Sheriff. Although his journey had been short his legs felt relief as soon as he was able to sit down on the cold hard floor.

'His horse was lost to the river and his men lost in the woods. When the Lord sent me to deliver you both he did not bring them as witnesses,' said the priest matter-of-factly. He patted Robin's shoulder reassuringly as if they had long been friends. 'No-one knows you are here. You are quite safe.' He moved over to the Sheriff. 'I greet you, my brother, with a holy kiss.' He said kissing him gently on the top of his head.

The Sheriff responded to this gentle greeting with muffled words that indicated that the Sheriff would like to return the greeting in exactly the opposite spirit.

'Thoughts of vengeance must be put aside, My Lord Sheriff,' mused the clergyman. 'This is a sacred space and, by law, any fugitive may seek sanctuary free from the fear of reprisal. Robin in the Hood is as welcome here as you are.'

At this the Sheriff began to swear with such vehemence he went entirely red; as if he were being boiled in his own anger. It was hard to tell if the fury was directed at him or their unusual host. Robin's amusement at his enemy's frustrations was interrupted with thoughts of his own band. Up until this moment he had been worried about the pursuing knights; but what if the outlaws found them first? Scarlet, John, Much, Tuck, Nasir and Marion. What if they came to the church? Then, the Sheriff of Nottingham could be captured and that could change everything.

Robin caught the Sheriff's unrelenting stare. He was now silent but Robin could see in his enemy's eyes that the Sheriff was thinking exactly the same thought. A crippled warrior alone and unable to lay hands on his bow or sword? For Robert too… this could change everything.

A curious murmuring caused them both to break their gaze. The priest was now kneeling in prayer. His eyes were shut and Robin, had the brief ignoble thought of stunning the cleric, retrieving his missing clothes and taking the sheriff swiftly back to the heart of the forest. The wounds on his legs immediately began to weep and his pain increased bringing him sharply back to the reality of his situation. He felt drops of warm blood run slowly down his left leg. Punishment or coincidence? Divine retribution aside the plan was surely ridiculous. Small though the Sheriff was, the winter weather would make their escape difficult even if he had been at full strength. The snow would make progress slow and the ice had already betrayed him once. Were it to do so again an unconscious priest would be unlikely to save them. No. For the moment they were stuck like wounded flies on butcher's tar.

The incantatory drone of the priest's prayer came to a sudden close. For the first time there was no sound save the crackle of the fire in the corner where Robin's wounds had been tended to. The near empty silence made the situation absolutely clear. The three men were utterly alone save for each other. Unlikely congregants in a desolate and forgotten church.

The priest opened his eyes and looked from Sheriff to outlaw and from outlaw to Sheriff.

'There was time when I was like you,' he said. It was not clear which of them he was referring to or, if he was talking to them both at the same time. 'I was a man of unquestioning violence who believed the world should be tamed by the sword or the bow.'

The Sheriff rolled his eyes for the second time that day. His brother the Abbot Hugo, occasionally had a tendency to sermonise and the Sheriff considered it his worst quality. This was an especially damning criticism for the Sheriff didn't really think his brother had any good qualities save, perhaps, naked ambition. Oh, and there was of course his greed which could always be counted upon.

'Once upon a lonely hillside,' the priest continued, 'a fierce and mighty angel did appear to lowly shepherds proclaiming the birth of the Prince of Peace.'

The Sheriff had heard this one before. In Canterbury. Something about Kings bowing the knee and giving up their wealth and assorted luxuries to the infant Christ. He had no idea how useful these things would be to a child but it did strike him that the pontificating preacher from whom he first heard the story, a greasy bishop with a love of grotesque gold rings, would be unlikely to part with his jewellery no matter what manner of baby he was confronted with. Yes, he had heard this one before and it always ended the same way – with a plea for coin and cash in order that the Lord's work may be done upon the earth. Good Father Blackteeth wanted a sackful of gold. Now, at least, this most miserable of days was finally about to make some wretched sense…

That was when the priest quietly rose and struck Robin hard across the face.

The Sheriff's eyes widened in surprise. Robin, who had been quietly listening and thinking on his wounds saw it coming but too late. He swerved his head out of the way; but not enough for the strike to miss entirely. The priest's fist was large and had a practiced strength and Robin could not withstand even the fraction of the blow. He fell sideways to the floor.

The priest's hands moved swiftly and he produced a rope from nowhere as if he were, in truth, some kind of sorcerer. With one hand he pushed a dazed Robin hard against the inside of a pillar whilst the other whipped the length of hemp around its outside. A mariner could not have worked faster and with more skill. Robin was soon tied fast to the stone column. The Sheriff grinned beneath his gag as Robin struggled against his own bonds. He could barely breathe let alone escape. The rope was of good quality and the eel hunting priest knew his knots.

'Forgive me, brother,' said the priest. 'I must leave you to confess your sins to each other whilst I attend to other matters. Were I not to restrain your body,' he explained, 'I fear the devil would prompt you to take the life of your neighbour. I will chastise myself for returning to my old ways but I knew you would not bridle yourself willingly.'

Robin opened his mouth to protest but soon found the tips of the priests gnarled and heavy fingers gently stopping his mouth.

'I struck you for love and not from anger, but that is still no excuse. Forgive me. Perhaps all three of us might consider, as Christmastide approaches, how we might ourselves sacrifice ourselves for peace? The priest smiled at the thought whilst the Sheriff grew uneasy again at this sudden moral appeal. This whole business would have been much easier if that familiar greasy bishop had pulled him out of the river instead of this unpredictable zealot. The church was, after all, always so much more manageable when it didn't take its own religion too seriously.

The priest smiled at them with an awkward expression, almost as if he had not been taught to place his lips together and so kept them strangely apart. It seemed as if he wanted to reassure his unlikely flock but both of his unwilling parishioners were left with the disturbing image of the black toothed rictus grin of a man who had planned a terrible fate and was entirely happy about it. As a parting gesture the priest removed the gag from the Sheriff's mouth and left them alone. The huge black figure disappearing into the shadows of the church.

Robin fixed his eyes on the Sheriff as he coughed and spluttered and flexed his mouth which seemed much relieved after its imprisonment. The Sheriff caught Robin's stare and surprisingly, in that moment, the Sheriff found himself completely speechless. Both men studied each other in a way that had not been afforded them before. Robin, in his mind, always pictured the Sheriff as a much older man. Robert, in turn, remembered Robin to have a considerably more vicious and vindictive countenance. How surprising it was to realise that they were, in fact, mere men. Both more boyish than their remembrances had led them to believe. Robin was used to keeping his own counsel and remained silent. How much time passed as they regarded each other was difficult to say. Eventually it was the Sheriff who broke the quiet in a sweet and icy tone.

'How wonderful it is to see you finally imprisoned. I knew this day would come but I must confess this wasn't quite what I had in mind.'

The Sheriff enjoyed his words. Every vowel was relished and every consonant hit. It clearly didn't take long for Robert de Rainault's tongue to recover its sharp strength.

Robin, meanwhile, said nothing. He was trying to work his shoulders to increase the space between pillar and rope. He used his breath to help expand and contract his chest. Small at first. Regular. Almost imperceptible attempts to shift his bones and gain ground between cord and column. He had learned the art from Scarlet who had found himself bound on more than one occasion.

'When Gisburne insisted on my joining him on some wild goose chase I really had no idea that the goose would turn out to be you. Yet, here you are, all trussed up and bled and ready for the fire. Do you think if I asked the priest nicely he would allow me to be the one to wring your neck?' said the Sheriff, who despite his ignominious position, had also found his superiority.

Robin did not respond. Talk can weary a man and it was already enough effort keeping his mind from the pain in his legs. He was attending to another matter. It was slow and Robin wasn't entirely sure his wrestle with the rope was achieving anything. Nevertheless, he pushed his shoulders out and then in, out and then in, out and then in. Eventually something must give.

'Doesn't hurt I hope?' smiled the Sheriff whose gaze was now focused on Robin's bloody legs. They were covered in a deep, dark red. Perhaps the outlaw's body would do de Rainault's work for him? Robin knew the blood was drying and it looked worse than it appeared; perhaps this might give him an opportunity? He took time from his efforts to loosen the rope. The Sheriff gaze was steadfast. They might not be hunting in Sherwood but Robin knew the feeling of the stalk before the chase and he was clearly the prey.

Time passed and Robin refused to directly engage. The Sheriff didn't appreciate the silence. He began to make popping noises with his mouth, as if this whole thing were a festivity and he was the wrenboy in charge. An amusement in winter.

'Do you like what you do?'

'And what's that?' snapped Robin. He was getting fatigued and the rope appeared to be resolute.

'Breaking the law. Is it thrilling? Is that why you do it?'

'I uphold the law. The only laws broken are those that shouldn't have been written in the first place.' Robin was surprised at his comment. He rarely had to explain his reasons for the people he served had always understood. Did the Sheriff honestly think he had chosen this life for entertainment?

'Ah... so, it's not the thrill. It's because you think you have the right to administer justice?' The Sheriff had met such men before and they usually found themselves contemplating their misplaced ideas in a prison cell or on a gallows platform.

'And you abandon justice when it suits you,' replied Robin.

Robert raised an eyebrow in surprise. Abandon justice? How could he, the High Sheriff of Nottingham abandon justice? He was justice. The King, himself, had appointed him to interpret and execute the laws of the land. To abandon justice would mean to abandon his position and his responsibility. Whilst he might be accused of many things, being work shy was surely not one of them. A peasant might complain about a judgement, it was after all what they were best at, but, if the High Sheriff made a ruling, then that ruling

21

was, by its nature, just. He worked hard and mostly he was rewarded with criticism. A weasel will always bite back at what it does not understand and the weasel in front of him was doing its best to draw blood.

The Sheriff leaned forward, or so far as his ropes would allow. He spoke with relish. Gisburne had always been a blunt instrument, useful in his own way, but he was a dullard and never one for truly interesting conversation. This caitiff in front of him, though he had caused so much trouble, was also the Sheriff's favourite kind of villain. He was a true believer. He always had the most fun disabusing zealots of their ridiculous self-righteous notions right before he had them killed. He wondered if he might have equal sport with that priest.

'You,' began the Sheriff, 'have no idea what it means to rule. You skulk about in a forest that does not belong to you. You order simpletons to rob and kill and then have the gall to think that you are a better representation of law and order than a duly appointed officer of the crown?'

'You only care for the rich, for the powerful. You've forgotten the people you're supposed to protect,' said Robin and began to work at his bonds once more. A French bloodied king might have put the Sheriff in Nottingham castle but he was called by a higher authority. He felt the ropes begin to give.

'Have I?' shouted the Sheriff in anger. His voice echoing through the church, 'Who ensures Nottingham has its grain reserves? Who hears the tedious arguments between the idiot goatherd and, his stinking neighbour, the fine fat master butcher? Who listens to the petty disputes over coin and candle? You? When the King requires soldiers to keep our lands secure from foreign foes I don't see you, wolfshead, calling to the scriveners or sending out the clarion call. Nor do I see you jumping up from the no-longer-a-Maid Marion's loose lap to offer your services to the King!'

Marion.

The thought of her interrupted Robin's focus. The very fact of his enemy now saying her name shot adrenaline, like an arrow, though his body. The pain in his legs disappeared.

'Much easier,' continued the Sheriff, 'to kill and roast venison that you haven't bred, on fires of wood you haven't grown. You talk of justice? You burn Nottingham because you can't build. You steal because you can't make. You rob because you don't earn and the only thing that lets you sleep at night, other than the stolen mead you've taken from honest merchants, is the spurious moral conviction that you bring justice.'

The words stung and, for a moment, Robin thought of Ailric, his father, and felt shame. Was he really just another kind of thief? He fought back with his words, 'The rich steal first so we steal it back to give it to the people that need it most.'

The Sheriff already knew this one was coming. He had not risen this high and this far without understanding his enemies.

'Yes, yes... minus the twenty-percent fee, for your trouble. My moneylenders do much the same thing but at least they have decency not to pretend it isn't in their own interest. It never fails to amaze me that you would happily shoot one of my men through the throat. A man who simply is carrying a sword so as to put food on his table. A man who earns no more than the ploughboys and swineherds you prefer to call "the people". The Sheriff spat the last word with such contempt that his spittle covered Robin's face. He continued, 'You slaughter them on a Saturday and celebrate on a Sunday. You, are what my dear departed father like to call a "spectacularly sanctimonious hedge-born plague-sore". You foul the earth, stink to heaven and all the while pretend you have the right to be there. You don't. You will be removed and God's good green wood will be all the better for it!'

The Sheriff relaxed back against the pillar, feeling, for the first time that day, a little merry. A physick from Suffolk had once prescribed him a course of regular morning vomiting in order to alleviate his black moods. It hadn't worked and said doctor soon found himself having to treat a bruised backside which, ironically, had cheered up the Sheriff no end. There was something to be said for the enormous relief that comes after the pleasure of eloquently unleashing bile on an unsuspecting stranger. He supposed he got that from his mother.

But then he noticed that Robin hadn't been listening. Robin had finally got an arm loose and was working to free the other hand. In panic, the Sheriff began to work at his own rope. He had tried earlier, of course, but soon found his wrist and legs quite burned at his attempts. He began again in earnest but they were both soon interrupted by the sound of hammering on the doors of the church.

'OPEN UP IN THE NAME OF THE KING!'

The knights had found a way to cross the river.

The priest had been preparing the water vessels when he heard the sound of the horses. His time in the heathen lands had attuned his ear to the subtleties of the noise of hooves and he discerned there were two riders approaching with fierce purpose. A single rider would imply that a messenger was coming. Two meant trouble. He sighed with a deep sadness. Would the land ever see peace? When would the rulers of this world abandon the sword for the ploughshare? When would the wolf lie down with the lamb?

He had been raised by a wolf. A man so vile and violent that, as a child, blood was as familiar to him as milk. He knew how to use his fists. It was as easy to him as breathing. A second language with his first being fear. Most violent men, he knew, operate out of fear. He had grown up afraid and, as he grew, so he saw his father shrink. What was to be done with such a man who, for so long, had ruled his petty kingdom with an iron hand? Certainly, were a certain act to be committed in the dark hours there would be none in the village who would weep. Everyone knew his father's character just as they chose not to intervene when he committed his acts of regular cruelty. It was as if some *fae* had cast an enchantment over their household. An invisible wall of shame. Shame at what was taking place and shame that everyone refused to get involved. No. There would be no tears, just a hole in the ground filled with the body of a tyrant. No one, he knew, would speak about such things, just as he also knew the invisible wall between his family and the rest of the village would remain. They were always to be outsiders at the heart of their community. In the end it was not by his hand that his father was vanquished, for the ale had done that for him, but, to his shame, he had often wished he had been the one to take his father's life. He had buried him alone and with no ceremony and, to his surprise, both he and his mother wept.

He had grown strong. When his mother died he found himself wandering the world and, on more than one occasion, had been set up upon by robbers. It was then he discovered that he truly did not care whether he lived or died. The fear had gone and his strength was increased by his wildness and rage. The men would lie dead, or near enough as to make no odds, and his purse grew fat. He was sixteen summers old and become a wolf himself. The roads were dangerous and so he found himself a sell-sword to various men. It was largely monotonous work and he longed for his masters to be attacked so that he might feel the beloved rush of blood to his head and heart. He was never vanquished for most robbers took to the bottle to help overcome their own fear before a skirmish. He wouldn't touch it. It had taken his father and, however much he longed for the peace a drink might bring, it would not take him. Even those who used the arrow were invariably too drunk or unskilled to shoot straight; besides they usually found that fear was enough to make a man hand over his goods. But not with him. He was no longer afraid of anything except, of course, the final Judgement.

He had had various masters and they all, bar one notorious rogue, had insisted on going to church. The clerics would speak in the incomprehensible popish tongue and none of it made any sense to the man who would rather hold a blade than hear a bible. Nevertheless the strange rituals compelled his attention. The bread that was broken and the wine that was blood. These things made sense to a man who knew all too well what it was to place your own body in harm's way in order that another may live.

A monk had once explained the rituals to him. The brother was tasked with providing Somerset honey, from the monastery, to the King's table. The honey had a particular sweetness and, it was rumoured, could prolong both life and virility. It had come to the King's attention that the bees feasted on certain flowers not to be found elsewhere in the land and His Majesty was determined to make use of their extraordinary qualities. The Crown paid the monks well for their merchandise and they in turn were extra vigilant in ensuring the honey would arrived safely. The sellsword found himself, during one particularly long and hot summer, spending many days trafficking with the monk from the country to the capital. He was not really needed for no one troubled such a small wagon; assuming its cargo to be of little consequence. The heat of that summer sapped time itself and the work grew long and lazy. The nights too stayed hot and sleep never seemed to come easy. It was during this time that the Monk was able to translate the mysteries of the church to the man that had, many times, slit throats, stabbed guts and stopped the breath of those who had crossed his path. He was greatly troubled that when his own breath was stopped he might be called to account for his deeds. He was not a man accustomed to the wash bowl and he often found himself staring at his fingernails. It seemed to him that they were always encrusted with the dark blood of his actions and the black soil of the graves he was often forced to dig. He could not remember a time when they had been clean. When the last of the honey was delivered he confessed all to his master who granted him absolution. The sellsword became a monk himself and took on the habit of peace until the time came when the honey-fed king called all true Christians to take up arms and reclaim the Holy Land for their Lord.

It had been a cruel time. As he fought he recalled the story of the river in Egypt that turned to blood. A judgement from God. When he found himself fighting in another desert, though there was little water, the sand was soon awash with a river of blood that he, himself, had wrought. He was a horseman of the apocalypse. He was a plague. He had wondered, on more than one occasion, if he were the devil himself. He realised the church had betrayed itself; whoring itself out for various kings and popes. He must, he thought, find a way to atone for its savagery and so he returned to the damp of England to begin again.

He heard the horses approach.

Men of violence come either for the Sheriff or the Outlaw. Instinctively, his had pressed against his habit and felt the metal underneath. He was wearing his Hauberk; not for protection but because it reminded him of the sins of his past and because the iron rings mortified his flesh. He opened a heavy chest in a dark corner of the church and by the time he heard the first knock he had hoods and gags in his hand. By the second knock he had re-gagged the Sheriff. The Sheriff had fought against the process but soon found the blade of the long thin knife, previously used to cut herbs, at his throat and so the prisoner had complied.

A third knock.

"Open up in the name of the King!' Ah. It was now clear the riders must be soldiers. Knights. Men from Nottingham Castle as oppose to the forest bandits. He must hurry. He moved quickly to gag the outlaw.

As Robin saw the man approach he thought about using his free arm to take the herb knife… but that was risky. He was still partially tied and the priest had the clear advantage. Instead, and with reluctance, he hooked his free wrist back under the rope and made a pretence of his frustration as the gag and hood went on. Darkness returned. Although he had lost his vision he was surprised that he seemed to be able to hear more clearly. The priest was leaving the prisoners to open the doors.

There would not be much time and, as the priest left to attend to the visitors, he doubled his efforts to free his other arm.

Stephen of Wallingford was rather wishing he had stayed in Wallingford. They had failed in their hunt to catch a deer when a notorious outlaw had interrupted their pursuit. They, in turn, had pursued said outlaw into a forest resulting in the crippling of a rather expensive horse, some minor cuts and bruises and with John de St-Calais' collision with that branch.

They had slung John back on his horse and tied him to the saddle. That meant, of course, another rider tethering themselves to John's horse and leading the animal back to the castle. Two men and three horses down. The odds were still easily in their favour but the merry hunt had become miserable and only the man Gisburne seemed keen to finish the matter.

Out of courtesy to their host they continued their pursuit. But, since John's cracked head, they rode with considerably more caution. And, as they all knew, caution would slow them down far more than the treacherous snow they were forced to ride in. The outlaw had vanished. It wasn't hard to track a man in the open snow but they weren't in the open. Every shivering tree branch and bush would shake snow atop of prints and the uneven terrain made the quarry's direction of flight difficult to ascertain. They were soaking too and this made things heavy and colder. With the earlier joys of mead and adrenaline beginning to wear off, their spirits soon gave up the ghost.

As the folly of the hunt became increasingly apparent so did the ill will of the knights. They began to moan first about the weather, then the task, then the wretched outlaw before finally turning on each other. Gisburne, aware that his companions had lost faith, eventually called off the hunt and they were almost back to Nottingham before he had stopped cursing and realised the Sheriff wasn't with them.

God's blood! Why is it that the Sheriff always seems to comfortably avoid the miseries of dealing with the scum of Sherwood?

'Where is my Lord Sheriff?' Gisburne asked the remaining knights. He imagined the Sheriff being back at his warm fireside thinking up insults for Gisburne's return.

The knights halted their horses and looked behind them. It was clear that, in their adventure, they hadn't paid any attention to the man who had provided them with coin and castle. Now the King's Officer was nowhere to be seen.

'Perhaps he has returned to Nottingham?' offered Stephen of Wallingford in the hope that this would speed the end of this ridiculous morning.

'What if the outlaw has him?' offered Nicholas Arrington. 'We should track back.'

Wallingford knew that Nicholas was hoping for a fat reward. He was a narrow-eyed fellow and always sharp when it came to the prospect of turning calamity into an opportunity to fill his pockets. For his own part he wished Nicholas had kept his mouth shut for Gisburne, clearly, now shared his desire to return home.

Gisburne hesitated. He could not ignore the possibility that his master had been taken but, at the same time, he was shivering and wet and beginning to get worried that the winter chill would lay him abed. If there was one thing he could not stand it was infirmity. Were he alone the matter would be simple. The Sheriff could hang. He was in no doubt that were the situation reversed De Rainault would not be sticking his neck out for Sir Guy's valued health and well-being. The knights were looking at him expectantly. He hadn't realised it before now but, for better and for worse, he was currently their leader. He rather liked the feeling of being in charge. It seemed to warm his bones.

'We ride back,' he said, 'with gold for the man who first spies my Lord Sheriff and ale for everyone else for their trouble!' He said this in his loudest and most confident voice and was rather disappointed that the Knight Bachelor didn't raise a cheer. Instead they turned the horses around trudged pathetically back through the forest.

After an hour or so they found their way back to the place where they had first set eyes on the hooded man. It was not long before they also found the tracks of the Sheriff's Charger. Salveyn, a Welshman, was the one who noticed that the horse had headed towards the river. Nicholas was discouraged for it was surely clear that the outlaws had not captured him and taken him into the forest for ransom. The river though? Surely he hadn't fallen in? Gisburne wondered if the Sheriff could swim. It didn't seem likely. He certainly hoped not. Perhaps it might fall upon Sir Guy to take up the position of High Sheriff of Nottingham?

The snow began to fall again erasing the tracks. The knights were growing increasingly restless. Gisburne made another decision. They must divide the company in order to better the chances of finding the Sheriff. Gisburne nobly nominated himself as the best man to return to the warmth of the castle and check the Sheriff hadn't simply returned home. The others rode North, South, East and West. It fell to Stephen and Nicholas to find a way of crossing the river and checking the curious church which marked the horizon. By the time they had found a patch of ice strong enough to hold them the rest of the Knights Bachelor had disappeared.

They had tied the horses to an outlying elm and risked crossing the ice on foot. Arrington went first. He had his greedy eye on the church. Both knew from their time in the Holy Lands that once you were inside a church it wouldn't be long before you found a thing worth stealing. In some of the more bitter campaigns it was not unknown for the Knights Bachelor to raid the Christian towns and later put the blame on the Moors. Wallingford didn't think much to their chances of finding anything other than dust in this poor place.

From the look of this malformed house of prayer the only thing they were likely to discover would be the loss of their time.

It was then that he saw it. A large patch of muddy grass by the river's edge.

It was curious. Surely the snow had fallen there. Why was it exposed? The ice had broken there and it could be that the flood water simply prevented the flakes from settling. It could be too that a man had crawled or been pulled from the river. He found his hand playing with the pommel of his sword. He had the itch. The itch had saved his life on more than one occasion. Something was wrong here and probably nothing a sharp blade wouldn't fix.

Suddenly he heard the cry of a raven as it flew fast and low over his head and alighted atop the church. Strangely, it sat comfortably among a murder of crows. A very ill omen if he paid heed to such things.

'What's keeping you, Master Snail?' shouted Arrington. He was nearly at the church door and clearly anxious to get inside.

'I've the itch,' replied Stephen drawing his sword.

'For this place?' Nicholas of Arrington was surprised. 'There's nothing here but field mice'.

'I've the itch,' Stephen repeated and Nicholas drew his sword. They had ridden together long enough for Nicholas to know what that meant. Although they were largely a company of fools who enjoyed foolish things, their sprightly living was largely supported by some very dark and dangerous deeds. Many blithe fellows had sought to join their band but none lasted that were not prepared to snap a neck as well as raise a glass. Stephen of Wallingford was usually reluctant to break a pate or too if he saw no sense in it but, when he had the itch, there was no man better to fight your corner. At Edessa he had watched

Stephen beat a man to death with the splintered leg of a fallen horse. When Death finally came with sickle and hourglass for Stephen of Wallingford it would not go easy for the reaper.

'Outlaws?' asked Nicholas.

Stephen shrugged. The itch didn't tell him of what manner a danger was, only that danger was surely there. They were both at the door now. Stephen was about to knock when Arrington stopped his hand.

'Put your sword to bed.' Nick said as he sheathed his own. 'Sanctuary.'

'Sanctuary!' replied Stephen in surprise, for Nicholas of Arrington had robbed more churches than any of them.

'We can't shed blood. Not in there. If there's a fool in want of a fight we'll have to draw them out first.'

'You-' Began Stephen but he was stopped by Arrington's determined expression.

'Some sins can't be forgiven, Wallingford. Put your sword abed unless it be outside the church.'

Stephen reluctantly put his sword back in its sheath. The itch was increasing. He felt naked and more than a little afraid. Nicholas nodded an acknowledgment of thanks. Stephen raised his fist and banged on the door of the church. He was a noble member of the Knights Bachelor and his voice carried authority as it was carried on the winter wind.

'Open up.' He demanded. 'In the name of the King!'

There was no response and so he banged again on the door. Harder this time.

"Open up in the name of the King!"

There remained a silence and Stephen began to feel a little foolish.

"Perhaps we should just try and force the doors?' Suggested a hopeful Nicholas. He found that a locked door was always an encouragement to a thief.

'OPEN UP IN THE NAME OF THE KING,' roared Stephen and, as if he had cast a spell, the doors finally opened. He found himself in the middle of a snow covered nowhere staring at a priest with black teeth.

The priest surveyed the knights. He was sad to note they obviously had the same contagion as his current beneficiaries. Alas, he could not help them. They were not part of the divine solution.

'We're looking for my Lord Sheriff,' said the Knight who had knocked.

The priest's mind wrestled with itself. He was no longer one for lying. That was one of his past sins. On the other hand the Lord's plans would not be achieved were the knights to discover his guests. So he simply raised his hand in benediction.

'*Quia apud te propitiatio est et propter legem tuam sustinui te domine,*' he began in a sustained and slow drone.

There wasn't time for this nonsense. Nicholas Arrington was now thoroughly sick of being wet through with snow and placed his hand on his sword to hurry the man along. He would not kill the priest in the sanctuary but surely no real God would judge a man for pulling a fool out into the snow and killing him there. Such a thing might be considered the natural way of things. Anyway the threat should be enough. A hand on a blade was usually enough to make people do what he wanted.

The priest however, suddenly seeming a good deal larger, placed his own giant hand on top of Arrington's wrist.

'Good Sir Knight, you must leave your weapons at the door. This is the House of God.' The priest's black teeth made a show of every word and Nicholas wouldn't have been surprised if this holy devil had been feasting on cockroaches. 'Your weapons must stay outside the sanctum.'

Nicholas Arrington had waited two weeks for his sword to be made and had no intention of leaving it to rust in the snow. Stephen, however, was unbuckling his sword belt. Arrington noticed he did not remove the knives in either of his boots.

'The Sheriff was pursuing an outlaw,' continued Stephen. 'Have you seen either of them?'

'All men are welcome into the embrace of the church be they outlaw or sheriff. But all must needs leave their weapons outside of a place of prayer. Can I pray for you, my brothers, that your endeavours may meet with God's approval and blessing?'

The priest was looking, without hostility, directly into Stephen's eyes. He showed no fear. Clerics usually avoided his gaze. They were so used to deference from the peasants they never seemed able to hold his stare. Perhaps this one could be trusted? On the other hand his itch was increasing.

'There's no one here,' Arrington said. The snow began to fall thickly now and he was as sodden as a swineherd. 'We'll not besiege you further, Father,' he said heading back to his horse. If there was one thing he couldn't stand about being a knight it was the bloody religion. Why was there so much standing around and doing nothing all the time? He held a healthy respect for the fear of God but he had no desire to spend his earthly days being bored into heaven. His plan had always been to have enough gold to pay others for pray for his soul. To his way of thinking this would make everyone happy. Especially himself.

Stephen of Wallingford, however, did not like a job half done and so began to approach the door. The priest was big but then, so was he, and unlike the priest, he had his two hidden knives that would enjoy being used should the need arise. The dolt Arrington was already leaving but, Stephen had to confess, he was probably right. Nothing here but field-mice and a lonely hedge-priest. A short look inside would be all that was needed to check that this dilapidated church wasn't really an outlaw's den. He stepped inside the sanctuary.

The sudden darkness briefly disorientated him. He was used to such places being filled with candles and incense. A sensuous reflection of eternal glories. In here there was only cold and dark and a fire burning in a dank corner. After a morning of his eyes staring at snow he found the sudden dark change made him blind.

It was then he heard a muffled cry.

He span round to confront the priest. 'Who do you have in here?' he demanded.

The priest took herbs from a pocket in his robe and offered them to the knight.

'For your protection, Sir Knight. There is a sickness that is spreading across the world. I myself once succumbed but the Grace of God did bring me safe out of the pit. I am treating them – perhaps you yourself might have contracted the sickness?'

The dried herbs, whatever they were, made Stephen feel light headed. From deeper inside he could hear the moans of some presumably sick peasants in need of Christian charity. His eyes began to adjust to the dark and he could see the priest had the remnants of other herbs down the front of his robe. Stephen of Wallingford was pretty sure that he did not have whatever sickness had befallen them and he didn't like the way the priest was closely staring at his face as if looking for signs of the contagion.

'Come in and be treated,' implored the priest moving his face so close to Stephen's that he briefly wondered if those black teeth would bite off his nose. The breath stank of the midden and Stephen was pretty sure any more time spent here would mean he was infected, too. No wonder the itch had been so strong.

It was plague! He was convinced it was.

With a firm arm, Stephen, pushed the pestilential priest hard aside and ran fast for the door. He had survived cudgel, sword, dagger and fire. He would be damned if a pox would take him to an early grave.

From behind his gag the Sheriff of Nottingham screamed for help. Screamed for the knight to come back but it was too late. The Knights Bachelor had fled from the church faster than if the devil himself were on their heels.

The priest was slightly disappointed. He noticed the knives in the man's boots as he ran.

It was now clear to him that the sickness had indeed spread and the men riding away from the church were positively riddled with it. The Lord had been merciful and revealed to him his own infection but, sadly, those fools were oblivious. It was too late. If they would not recognise their sorry condition then, alas, he could not help them.

He re-entered the church and shut the doors. He did not trouble to bar them this time for the danger was now surely past. He removed his gown revealing the bloody and worn chain mail he was wearing as penance and returned to those who had been delivered unto him. They did not appear to be at peace.

The outlaw seemed a little unnerved at the sight of the priest's bloody armour. How strange that a man of blood would seem so discomforted by the suffering of another. Perhaps, there was hope for him? The Sheriff, meanwhile, had managed to free at least one of his body parts: his tongue. The gag was now half off and the priest reflected how interesting it was that the first thing the Sheriff tried to free was his mouth. It was exactly the kind of thing the serpent in Eden would have done. He noticed that for the first time, since he had pulled the rogue from the river, the Sheriff was smiling.

'Now... look, Father, what you have in front of you is an opportunity. I'm willing to overlook this... treatment of me because you did, after all, save my life.'

'Any man that wishes to save his life must also lose it,' replied the priest.

Despite his high office Robert was used to finding himself completely powerless with the assorted nobility that he was often forced to consort with. He was not, however, used to being spoken to as if he were an illiterate peasant. 'Are you threatening me?' accused the Sheriff.

The priest looked surprised at the idea. 'Why would I pull you from the river only to threaten you?' asked the priest.

'You think we're sick.' interrupted Robin. Behind his back he now had both arms free now and was waiting for his moment.

'The sickness has spread across the world, yes,' the priest said sadly. 'It took me and nearly claimed me as it has so many others. Now, like sin itself, it has you in its grip. The outlaw is infected by his nature but even you, my Lord Sheriff, even you now have it in your blood.'

'And you have treated us with kindness and with skill,' said Robin softly. A quiet voice can make a man come close and he needed the priest to be as close as possible. 'You have done your part. Perhaps you have cured us already?'

The Sheriff realised something that made him feel vaguely queasy. Both he and that wretched master of the bow wanted the same thing. Without an agreement they had implicitly formed an uneasy alliance. No. He would rather die at the hands of this petty pope than work with that wooded wastrel. In his experience men usually could be moved by any number of things – women, glory, fear – to name but a few. In his experience, however, the most useful lever in a tricky situation was coin. A coin had the king's head on it for a reason. Coins commanded action.

'If it's money you want, I can get it. The price on his head for a start, plus a prize from my own personal purse. You can buy yourself a better parish or perhaps settle yourself somewhere a little more... civilised.'

The priest looked at the Sheriff in disgust. He seemed genuinely angry. 'Mammon' he spat!

The Sheriff wasn't really sure what a 'mammon' was but, judging from the priest's expression, he was pretty sure it wasn't a compliment. Manoeuvring this holy fool might require a little more subtlety.

'You said I was brought here for a purpose,' noted Robin. 'You said I had to recover my strength. I think your hands have done marvellously well. I feel renewed. Your cures have surely worked '

'You cannot be cured. Only delivered,' the priest said, looking back at Robin. 'I was not speaking of bodily disease but a malady of the soul. You are men of violence. You are infected with it. You infect others with it. The whole world has tumbled into the sickness of the sword.'

The Sheriff wanted to roll his eyes again. Truly, could any more ridiculous nonsense beset a man on a single day? A churchman wanting them to put down their swords and take up what? A daisy-chain?

The priest continued; his eyes staring uncompromisingly at the outlaw. 'I saw it worst in Palestine. There I slew the pagan, heard his screams and washed myself in his blood until... until the only thing that would stop my hearing his screams would be to kill more and more and more until I could no longer separate one death from another.'

For a brief moment the large priest reminded him of Will Scarlet who, in his darker moments, would unleash a traumatic storm of hateful words and malicious memories to all around him. In those times, Robin had noted, it was almost as if Will wasn't really there. That his spirit had been taken away to some other nightmarish realm. The priest was no longer talking to them, for he was in another dreadful place. He was talking to himself.

Then the priest fell silent. The prisoners did not dare speak but only watch as their captor appeared to be recalling moments from a terrible past. One of his arms was shaking and fresh blood dripped from within his grossly fitted hauberk and fell to the stone floor. Robin wasn't sure how long this episode lasted but the time felt heavy until it finally passed. The priest suddenly blinked and moved his head. He smiled benignly at his new companions.

'By the grace of God I was able to escape the sickness of the battlefield and serve the Lord but, on returning to my once peaceful home, I then discover men like you spreading the sickness here.' There was more resignation than judgement in his voice but it was not without a tone of warning. 'This… cannot be allowed to continue.'

'You want us to repent?' the Sheriff asked with incredulity. He had dealings with many people in the church – not least his obnoxious brother the Abbot Hugo – but none of them took that doctrine seriously.

The priest smiled. 'The eels I catch cannot repent. Their desire to swim away is in their fallen nature; just as yours is to resort to bow and blade. I will make an atoning sacrifice,' he said, looking longingly at his newly prepared altar. 'You will be at peace. The land will be at peace. The people need no longer fear being caught in your endless battles.'

Robin and the Sheriff looked at each other as they slowly began to realise what was about to happen.

The priest continued in a voice as gentle as spring, 'I will save you from your evil nature by cutting your throats on the holy table and I pray that this sacrifice will be acceptable unto the Lord.'

Much the Miller's son hated grinding wheat. When he had found himself a man of the forest he thought his grinding over. Except that, these days, in the cold of the winter caves, making arrow heads in the smoke and dark seemed an even worse labour. His hands were often burnt by the makeshift forge and his lungs were filled with the smoke of burning metal. He longed for summer, for warmth and lazy days by the river.

It had been his turn to hunt but, despite his young eyes, his bow hand was not as sure as the older men and, on more than one occasion, he had failed to bring meat home. He felt guilty. They were running into the emergency supplies and, if things carried on, they would be forced to suck leather belt and shoe to stave off the pangs of hunger. It had been his turn to hunt but he was worried he would fail again and, like as not, Scarlet would give him an earful of noise if not something harder. Marion intervened and Robin, though he was due rest, had gone once again in search of food.

The other men were looking at him as if he were a burden. Even Tuck seemed to have lost his smile. They were all tired and the snow and the dark seemed to be poisoning everyone's mood. He tended to his work and tried to avoid the sure feeling that he wasn't really made for this life. Perhaps he should be back at the mill? Perhaps the only reason he was here was because his step-brother protected him? He was no warrior. He was a poor-tom-beggar-by-day and doing nothing but making it harder for everyone else.

He coughed metal smoke from his lungs and caught another look from Nasir who was trying to conserve his energy by sleeping. Nasir had been on early watch but, with Much's constant spluttering, he had not been able to settle. That was when he burned his hand. He had been so busy looking at the Saracen he had let his tired hand drop near the molten metal. Gloves or not the fiery metal burned and he cried out in pain.

'Stop that mealy mouth, boy!' said John who was constantly worried they would be discovered in this place. When the days grew dark and long so John's mood grew sombre and black.

Tears began to fill in Much's eyes, although whether they were caused by the fire or his feelings of shame it was hard to tell. 'Why don't you stop *yours*, John Little!' he found himself shouting back in anger and, with that, he left the forge, abandoned his gloves and ran out of the cave.

'Much?' cried Marion as he pelted past her, but he ignored her. His face was burning red as much as his hands. Out into the morning he ran and plunged his hand into the snow. He felt a little relief before the cold began to bite. He pulled his hand out: it did not seem a bad burn. In fact, his slender fingers were already turning blue. He was sobbing loudly now. Like a child.

'Much? What's wrong?' Marion's voice was coming close. He wanted to be hugged, to be held but as her voice came closer he realised he did not want her to seem him crying like an infant. So, he ran...

Running seemed to help. He could cry without fear and the crisp air seemed to clear the harsh metallic smoke from his lungs. He ran harder. His legs becoming more water-soaked with every stride. He didn't care. He just wanted to be away from all this. He ran east after Robin. He needed his brother. His pain drove him fast and, in truth, he did not fear being caught or of falling on icy ground. He ran east and without care until he saw the fallen deer. It lay bloody on the ground and, immediately, he began to salivate. Roast deer! Robin must be close! He could not see the arrow in the animal's flank. Instead, it was lying next to the beast. The hunter had clearly pulled it from the animal. With his work done why then had he left it behind?

That was when he heard the men on horses charging back into the forest. His heart leapt into his mouth and he ran deeper into the forest. He could hear them charging through bracken and brush. His hands found a young oak and without much thought he realised he was climbing furiously up a conveniently placed series of branches. His frame was light and this work was easy. Soon he found himself above the forest floor looking down as various knights rode past. Two, then three. They did not see him but rather seemed to be looking for something. Perhaps it was they who had killed the deer. Who then had pulled the arrow from the beast?

The knights turned and doubled back under the tree. They seemed a little drunk and more than a little excited.

'This way!' shouted a familiar voice. It was Gisburne. Much's stomach turned. He wished he had brought his bow. He felt in his pouch. All he had were hazelnuts. They were poor things; small and past their best. He took a couple and threw them into a nearby bush. A pair of goldcrests flew sharply from their nest, protesting loudly as they flew into the air. All the knights turned and, without saying a word, they charged towards the birds. Something surely must have caused them to fly!

Gisburne and the three knights rode away but Much could hear other knights coming towards him. He could play the same trick but that would leave him without food. Perhaps they would charge on? He waited fearfully but it wasn't a knight he saw next. It was Robin, stumbling back near the deer. He had doubled back from Gisburne's knights not realising the other half of the party were heading straight towards him. Much wanted to shout and warn him from his position atop the oak but that would reveal his position and the knights would surely surround them both. The sounds of hooves came close. A single rider had seen the outlaw and was keen to run him down. Robin was already running again but there was no doubt the knight would soon be upon him. There was only one thing to be done. Much flung himself down to a lower branch and as the knight rode under the tree he kicked the fellow hard and watched him tumble from his horse. John de St-Calais fell hard from his horse, his pate bloodied by Much's harsh heel.

The knight's horse careered off into the forest and Robin was gone. Much leapt from the oak leaving the branches shaking snow on top of the injured warrior. He ran in pursuit of Robin. Behind him he could hear more knights arriving to find the body of their man apparently having been knocked clear of his steed by a shivering oak branch.

He ran deeper into the forest after his brother. Though the snows made it difficult to tell if he was actually heading back into Sherwood or merely skirting its edges. He rambled around for what seemed like hours. He could not find a trail and at one point found himself back at the fallen deer. His stomach gave him pangs and he wondered if he should simply try and get the meat back to the caves. He hit his forehead hard with his palm.

Stupid, stupid, stupid dolt! he growled inwardly.

A bloody trail leading to the secret place. What a fool you be, Much the Miller's son. At least he was wise enough not to try and eat the meat raw. He did, however, cut a portion and place it in his pouch. At a safe point he might be able to cook and eat the meat later. Besides, he did not know how long it would take him to find Robin. Occasionally, he would hear voices and would scramble to find a hiding place. He found hoof-prints and even a crossbow bolt at the base of a sycamore. It looked expensive and he placed it in his boot. He had always been a magpie of sorts. Much the Magpie feathering his nest! The idea made him laugh. His merriment was interrupted by the sound of distant voices. He clapped both his hands over his mouth. They were talking. A Welshman was talking about a river and the Sheriff. Was the Sheriff here too? He did his best to move as far as possible from any trace of the pursuing knights.

When the sun rose higher to greet the day he realised he needed help. He could not find Robin, who had probably already returned to their fellows and he was now numb with cold. He made his way hopefully back to the caves but found, once again, he had no idea where he was. It had been an hour or more since he had anything from the knights and had begun to relax and think himself safe. Except he wasn't. He was truly lost. Eventually the landscape again began to seem more familiar and, indeed it was, for he found himself again confronted with the deer. He was back where he started! He wanted to cry again. There was only one sure way to head back swift and that would be out of the cover of the canopy. It would not be safe but with the sun's progress gradually west he could figure things out by following the tree-line.

When finally he stepped out of the forest. He heard two different knight's voices.

'Open up, in the name of the King!'

He fell flat. Mercy! There was a church across a frozen river. Two knights were hammering on the doors. There he would find shelter. He could raise a fire and dry himself and cook the bloody meat from his pouch. He watched and waited. A monk or a priest of some bishopric or other came out of the church. Another mercy! Once the knights were gone he could seek aid from the cleric. Eventually, the priest appeared to giving them a blessing and the one knight scrambled uneasily across the ice. Ah! So that's where they crossed. The other went into the church but soon returned and followed in the footsteps of the other. The second knight mounted his horse and rode hard to catch the first. Much lay there awhile to make sure they were gone before beginning to make his way to the ice where the knights crossed. His spirits lifted as he scrambled fast across the snow happily heading into the safe and sure welcome the priest would, no doubt, bring.

Piers Swynbourne had a man and that man had a sack. They had returned swiftly to Nottingham Castle to find the cocksure Guy of Gisburne sitting in the Sheriff's chair, cup in hand, listening to Nicholas of Arrington.

'Well, he must be somewhere!' roared Sir Guy who was doing a fairly good impression of a ranting Robert de Rainault.

'Sir Guy, we found nothing but a miserable church filled with maladies. We did not stay long,' shrugged Nicholas.

'God's wounds! Is there no man here capable of finding my Lord Sheriff? I thought you were knights!'

'Knights. Not errand boys,' spat Stephen of Wallingford who was beginning to tire of Gisburne's petulance.

'Mercenaries do as they're told,' said Gisburne looking hard at Wallingford. If the man wanted a brawl he would oblige.

'We're guests, Gisburne, of the Sheriff of Nottingham, not some of your peasants-at-arms to be badgered into battle,' opined John de St-Calais from his position at the fireside. His head was bandaged and he had more than a little mead since he had awoken. 'Besides, a mercenary is paid to fight and not roam the country like some itinerant friar.'

'Well, then, perhaps his guests would oblige me and find their host,' retorted Gisburne angrily. He had honestly expected Robert to be at the castle and his long absence was now beginning to concern him. The joys of leadership were wearing thin; especially as now it appeared that this rabble were turning against him.

'We didn't lose him.' said Gilbert de Grant absently. He was looking at the maid who had bandaged John's head and who was now bringing him some broth. He wondered if she might be available for other duties.

'But we may have found him,' said Piers stepping forward. The knights turned to look at him. Most of them hadn't been aware Swynbourne had returned.

'Piers! I thought you in Scotland you've been gone so long!' cheered Gilbert.

'Scotland, will only ever see my backside,' Piers replied with a smile. He was in a good mood. The others had clearly failed whereas he had a man and that man had a sack.

Gisburne sighed with some relief. He strapped on a grin. 'Swynbourne! Well now, you're a fellow who brings good cheer. What news?'

Piers shoved the man forward. The man was warmly dressed but he was a poor sight. Lank hair and with the grease of the river about him. There was not a bit of colour in the man's garments and he reminded Gisburne of something you might find in a pig's trough.

'My Lord...' began the man, nervously.

'Speak up, mumblecrust!' snapped Sir Guy.

'My Lord, I work the river,' continued the man, clutching anxiously at his sack. He was trying to speak more loudly but the soldiers that surrounded him were making him nervous.

'God in heaven, Piers. What did you do to my Lord Sheriff? He looks like a drowned rat!' shouted a somewhat confused John de St-Calais from his fireside. Gisburne shot him one of his more filthy looks. The branch had clearly done more damage than was first thought and, if he didn't shut up, he fancied he might have to deal the fellow a second blow.

'Quiet!" roared Gisburne. 'Let the thing speak.'

'I work the river, my Lord, east of Sherwood. Takes the fish when they're kind enough to bite. Except this morning comes a prize that I never wuz expectin.'

'You found... his body was in the river?' Gisburne's heart was beating fast now. Was it true? Could it be that Robert was dead?

'No. Not no body. Least not nothing human.'

'God be praised. He's found a mermaid!' cried out John Salveyn who, up until this point, had been scoffing a bread filled with yesterday's mutton. There was never any reason to speak unless the opportunity for a jest presented itself and this fisherman had unwittingly obliged. Arrington laughed. Gisburne, however, picked up a nearby dish and threw it hard at the knight. It narrowly missed Salveyn's face which now expressed such a state of innocent shock that Arrington and de Grant laughed even harder.

Stephen of Wallingford, however, was not laughing. Stephen had his hand on his sword and was ready to rush at Sir Guy. No one insulted a knight without paying for it. The question was merely as to whether it would be now or later.

Piers intervened. 'Tell Sir Guy what you found.'

Stephen of Wallingford relaxed his grip. Later then. Sir Guy would pay for his insolence in the time that was to come. The fisherman, meanwhile, continued his tale, 'A body comes, my Lord. Indeed it do. But not no man nor no girl neither... but an 'orse. Comes a floatin' down to my bank. What's this? sez I. And I takes a fancy to the saddle and the like. Calls my boy, I do. Down 'ee comes, and twixt him and I, we pulls the beast, water and all, onto the shore. Takes some doing but we does it.'

'You have the Sheriff's horse?' enquired Sir Guy.

'Horse stays where she lays. Not good for eating not now she's been in Jenny Greenteeth's maw. River likes to taste but she don't like to eat. Spits 'em all back, she do. No, the beast will rot but, sez I to my blood, 'Boy', I say. 'Fetch my bone cleaver for we'll have us this leather for market and that twill feed us more'n yon 'orse.' So he duz, and we do, and off to market is we, only on our way, Sir Knight finds us.' The fisherman gestured to Piers.

Swynbourne shrugged. 'I asked them if they had seen the Sheriff or anything unusual.'

'Sez I. T'aint every day you fish up an 'orse'. 'An 'orse?' sez ee. 'Aye', sez I, 'an here be its saddle. The fisherman opened his sack and pulled out the saddle. It was clear the man was telling the truth. 'All fine work as you and your eyes can see.' And sez, sir Knight, 'that be the Sheriff's saddle.' And I say, 'then he be in the water like as not.'

'Drowned?' asked Guy, breathlessly.

'Could be. He doan come with his 'orse tho.'

Piers interrupted. 'We rode to the bank where this rascal had broken the ice. Nothing came. So I asked the fellow if there was anywhere else we might find the body.'

'They do fall in the river upaways. The ice is soft in places up river. Good spots for fishin' when winter bites. Least ways the ones I is allowed to put in my net.'

'What do you mean, the "ones you are allowed"?' asked Gisburne, leaning in.

'Tell, Sir Guy!' barked Piers, giving the fisherman a shove.

'Well, Sirs, they do say the river belongs to herself and so any man can dally with her if he's not afeared to try his luck. Exceptin' when he came.'

'He?' Gisburne had caught a scent. He might not be as learned as some at court but he always had a nose for a hunt. He had to pursue this quarry. 'Who is this "he"?'

'Demon come. From the pit. Black of tooth and black of hand. It was summer and one eve the moon gone blood red and we reckon that's what done it. Not that we knew what 'ee were when first he smiles, 'God be with you.'

'A demon?' cried out Arrington, scornfully. But the rest of the room was quiet. It was most likely folk foolery but, with such matters, it was sometimes better to err on the side of caution.

'He came with rocks and iron. Rebuilt that church with his bloody hands he did. Some of us helped and he paid us in coin. We thought him a friar exceptin' he never held no mass nor said no prayers e'en when he be asked.' The fisherman had lost his sense of fear and found his words coming more easily now. 'Church him do finish and some of us do say it might be easier to cum there than go aways to Marten. Demon says to uz we can't come to chapel lest we infect holy ground. 'You have it your way', we sez, "for it makes no matter to uz," and we leaves him to his queer ways and do seek God where we always dun. "Alls well", sez we, and all was well until Putnam dallied in yon river.'

The room remained quiet. Stephen of Wallingford was beginning to wish he had looked more carefully inside the church. He looked over at Arrington who was looking sheepish.

"Putnam was an eel-man. I'm more for nets but he could take a willow and make some fine baskets that would hold elvers in, right happily. Strong he was, on account of his work, and so he does gone fish where he always do right by that church. Putnam comes back one day and he do tell uz that yon demon had told him the river do belong to God and that hell-bound folk like Putnam got no business taking what do not belong. Seems that Master Blacktooth got his own fishin' and he doan like Putnam puttin' in. We say, "Putnam, best you listen to mother church and find yourself another spot." "I will not," sez 'ee, "For 'twas the place of my father and twill be the place for my son." We thought maybe the priest might be softer than he do look and maybe find another spot for himself for Putnam speaks fair. All shall be well. But, Putnam goes back to yon church only he do take his cudgel. Sez we, 'Putnam, why do you take that stick of yours?' Sez Putnam, "I'll not be moved by that fellow, and if it come to it, I'll knock some heavenly sense into him," and off he goes. 'Cept he don't come back.'

'What happened?' asked Gisburne. The knights had moved closer now. Even John de St-Calais had abandoned his fire to better hear the story. The fisherman's mouth had gone dry and was looking plaintively at a jug of water on a nearby table. Piers saw the glance, poured mead into a cup and pressed it into his hands. The fisherman swiftly drank it down.

'Thank 'ee, masters. Well, Putnam's wife not seen 'im and her bed is cold and so she do come knockin' late. She's worried that Jenny Greenteeth has drunk up her 'usband like I done gone drunk that wine. "No", sez I, "for he knows his way around water." And we all knew it, then. Yon Priest and Putnam must have set to and who came the worst of it who's to tell? "Go find him!" pleads she and, though it be midnight, we dress for church and the

42

cold. Me, there is, my boy and my brother. And we takes nothing with us but ourselves."

At this, the Fisherman opened his hands to show the knights they were empty. There was something in his tone that made the assembly want to reach for their swords.

"She comes too a course, only a knife she do bring. Same ways her folk, her Father and Putnam's brother too do bring blade and bow. Sez I, "best be leaving them instruments here. Trouble is already come and none of us need beg for more.' But they doan listen and in their fear and fury they do bring a sharp reckoning to the sanctuary. We gets there and the mercy of the moon lights uz a path. All is quiet but not all is well for when we knock we hear the cry of carrion crows. A church is a place for the living but when Friar Black-a-mouth do open those doors all we can smell is death. 'I knew you would come,' Sez 'ee. 'Where is my husband?' says she. 'At peace,' replies the devil with a smile and gestures to yon altar. Then, as gentle as a lamb, he moves out of the church and into the night. None of us do stop him for we see Putnam there on the table. Runs to him, she do, though her Father tries to stop her. My hand is over my boy's eyes for no one should see Hell's work. My brother, then, puts his hand hard on my shoulder for, as 'ee sez, "my legs broke right from under me". "No," Sez Putnam's brother and ee's not spoken since. Not a word more. Seeing Putnam stopped his tongue stronger than a witch's curse. Silence for him and I pray God his voice come back. Screams, though, does she. Putnam's wife is all noise. Scream and scream and scream filling the whole cursed church with it. A song of pain it were.'

At that the fisherman sat down on a stool. It was an insult to the company. A commoner taking from nobility what had not been offered; but none of them objected. They realised he was slightly trembling. His story had become a memory and the memory was shaking his body.

"Her father done pick her up and, though she do kick and scream, he's taking her off and out. "Take the boy," say I to my brother whose recovered his legs, " Take the boy home," and that he do and right swift. His brother though do stop still. Him's as frozen as the river is now. 'We must bring him,' sez I though the sight of Putnam makes my guts right sick. And he comes, as I leads, and together we get close to where Putnam lays. Crack! Comes a sound that makes us both leave our skins. I stepped on a thing. An eel cage. Putnam's fine work. I did break it. No. T'was not so, for now I sees there's more'n one. All of his cages are here; only now they're broken and splintered and arranged like firewood around the table. And I think, 'ees done it! This devil has laid out these baskets like flowers round a grave. And 'tis a kind of grave for there lies Putnam naked as a babe. Clean and washed and white he is, save for where his throat has been cut and his blood drained off. Now, I seen the dead before and I seen the dead since but I never seen a dead man looked so cared for. What could this mean? He was as neat as a knife and sees I then, in his hands, his cudgel. Broken it was and each of his fists held a piece. All was quiet but not all was still for I see, even in death, his tongue is moving back and forth, back and forth, back and forth. I think it the light playing tricks but, no, though it be night, his tongue is moving, plain as day. There's no sound but it's like Putnam is calling out from the grave. Justice? Sorcery? Then, God in heaven, hell comes. For then I see it, not one tongue but two, then three. Multiple tongues writhing from within his mouth. More'n three now. How many tongues can 'ee have, think I? Then, out from his mouth, comes a tongue at me. Long it is and leaves Putnam it does, slithering across his chin and out onto the floor. That's when it dawns. When I seen what 'ee gone done. The Demon had killed Putnam and laid him bare upon his table. Cut a throat and did for him. Then, 'cos devilry always do want more, it had done something else."

There was a long and uneasy silence as if the fisherman couldn't bear to continue with the story. It was Stephen of Wallingford who spoke first. 'What had the devil done?'

"He… " continued the fisherman, "He had stuffed the body with eels."

There was an audible outtake of breath from the knights. Gisburne was now wondering what miserable fate had befallen the Sheriff if it was indeed true that this monstrous cleric had claimed him instead of the river. All the company appeared troubled. Gilbert De Grant was crossing himself and muttering a prayer to the saints.

"Then, from out of the shadows comes the fiend. Putnam's brother draws his sword though he be in no shape to swing it. Besides, think I, there's no blade on earth that will cut a creature from the pit. So I just show it my hands, like this.'

The fisherman made the same gesture as before, revealing his hands to be empty.

"Say I, 'We come for the body.' Demon sez, "He is at rest." That's a-when Putnam's brother drops his sword and begins to cry. Say I to the devil, 'We are men of sorrow. We want no bloodshed. In Jesu' name let us live.' Say the thing, 'take up no sword and you shall live'. 'Amen,' sez I, showing him my hands and Putnam's brother, he do likewise. "Take the body and go in peace,' says the creature all soft like the serpent he is. Then, 'ee steps aside into the darkness. Gone. That be the last time I saw him and I pray God it be the very last. Then, we take Putnam home and put him aground. French Priest from Marten come and do what's right and lays him properly afore God. He don't ask what happened and we don't tell. We just fish the river. Us in our part and the devil in his.'

'You think he has the Sheriff?' asked Gisburne.

'He could be in the river,' began Piers, 'but if the ice is soft by this demon's church, as this man says, then the church is a good place to look.'

There was a palpable sense of unease in the room. None of them were saints and the thought of fighting a demon would not end well. Indeed, the Devil always claimed his own.

'We already looked in the church!' moaned Nicholas of Arrington. 'He wasn't there. Ask Stephen.'

The knights turned and looked at Stephen. He wasn't their leader. The Knights Bachelor didn't have a leader unless you counted self-interest. He was, however, the most trusted of all the rogues that rode under their banner.

'What say you, Wallingford?' asked Sir Guy. 'Could he be in the church?'

'He could. The priest scared us off with stories of plague. We should ride there now.' Said Stephen plainly.

'I'll not fight the Devil.' said Salveyn.

'Nor I,' said Gilbert De Grant.

'Nor I,' replied Stephen, too, 'for there is no devil, nor no demon, nor any dragons, nor *fae*-folk, nor anything else from a grandmother's tale. There is just a madman in a church—'

'He's big,' interrupted Arrington.

'So am I,' finished Stephen.

'If he's done anything to Robert then I'll do more to him than fill his mouth with eels,' cried Gisburne angrily. The blood was beginning to rush to his head. It was a feeling he adored.

'My Lord, it's not safe.' Said the fisherman. 'He is not of this world.'

'It might not be safe,' put in Arrington. 'He may not be the devil and he might be telling the truth about the plague.'

'First man in can see what's true,' said Piers. 'I'll do that for a larger share.'

'It's yours, Swynbourne,' said Guy, 'In fact, take up that man's sack. For if we kick the devil, escape the plague and save the Sheriff, you shall surely fill that bag with Nottingham gold!'

'No, my Lords, please...' begged the fisherman. Had they not heard a word he had said?

Gisburne threw the man a silver coin. 'For your trouble, fisherman. We thank you for it. God willing, it look like you may have helped us catch a Sheriff.'

45

The priest was attending to the altar. He was humming a plainsong as he covered the table with a spotless white cloth. He had extinguished the fire for he did not want the cloth spoiled by the smoke.

Elsewhere, Robin had freed one arm and was beginning to work at the other. The sun was higher now and light came through the wooden shutters that covered the holes which made for windows. There was no glass here. This was a poor man's church. The Sheriff could see the outlaws progress and found himself frantically licking his lips. An odd response, he thought, for it was not as if he wanted to eat the fellow.

'Wolfshead! Wolfshead!' he ventured in firm tones that were soft enough not to attract the priest's attention.

Robin ignored him. There was not much time.

The Sheriff continued, 'It gives me no pleasure to say this but I am most sincerely desirous of your help!'

'Help you? And when was my Lord Sheriff ever in need of my help?' replied Robin. The knot was too tight to unpick and so he was having to fray the thing against stone.

'Is letting an innocent man die the justice you were talking of earlier? Set me free!' spat the Sheriff. His stare so fierce his eyes were bulging now more than usual. He was willing the bandit to listen. Magical thinking.

The rope snapped and Robin of Sherwood was finally free. 'You're hardly innocent,' he said staggering to his feet. But he was light-headed and the wound dressings began to break. His legs gave way and he fell hard onto stone.

'And you're hardly standing. If you don't free me and let me help you how do you expect to escape?' said the Sheriff.

'I don't trust you.'

'Then we will both be dead,' shrugged the Sheriff. He was good at shrugging. He liked the way a good shrug infuriated those he talked to.

Robin thought for a moment. Reluctantly he began to drag himself across the ground and begin to free his enemy.

'There's a good boy,' breathed the Sheriff.

'You're not safe yet.' hissed Robin into the Sheriff's ear.

'Neither are you, Loxley.'

The Knights Bachelor were dangerous when they were drunk but, when they were sober, they were absolutely deadly. They had redressed in warm clothes and full armour. This time they were not hunting a deer in the forest and so had no need to travel light. Horses were watered and fed. Swords were re-honed with a steady and well-practiced use of a stone. Quivers were restocked with bolts and crossbow springs oiled and tested for a quick sharp satisfying snap.

They drank water and not ale for they intended to be sharp about their business. The fisherman was insistent about not guiding them back to the church. He did not want to see the demon again lest they all end up in hell but Swynbourne dragged him to his horse with the use of curses, knife and the threat of the noble Knights Bachelor paying a bloody visit to the man's son.

The plan, if it could be called that, was simple. They ride to the church. They break the doors down with fire and force. The priest would be pulled from the place and put to the sword. The Sheriff, should he remain alive, would be saved. No blood would be spilled in the Sanctuary for that would bring doom upon them all. Outside, however, they would fill the wretched river with it. And, if heaven did smile upon them, and the Hood and his fellows, interrupted their work, then the Knights Bachelor would work such a slaughter that their name would become legend. They were fury. They were plague. They were death come a-riding to put the King's enemies under turf and stone.

Sir Guy of Gisburne rode out first but the Knights Bachelor could not give a fig for the pretty-boy as he barked out orders. They had no leader. Except every man, when in doubt, looked to Stephen of Wallingford who rode hard and close behind Sir Guy.

'Stay back, Wallingford!' commanded Sir Guy, as they rode. Stephen's larger steed was making his own horse skittish and hard to control on the icy ground.

'Beg Pardon, *my Lord.*' Shouted Stephen with an edge in his voice, as he continued to press his horse hard and close. He was excited by the business at hand. Church. Priest. Sheriff. Then, afterwards he had an extra task of his own. Sir Guy of Gisburne had insulted a Knight Bachelor and Stephen of Wallingford would see to it that Sir Guy of Gisburne, in the confusion of the day, would find himself on the end of his sword.

The boy had run hard and fast to Wickham. He had spent his life living slow on a river bank and was not used to running.

The day had started early, it always did, but winter made things earlier still. The fire had to be made and when the air was this cold he would wake shivering; keeping moving was the only sure way to keep from turning blue.

His father, grumbled, got his nets and sack and readied himself for the morning. There was dry bread, which the boy softened in ale, before they both chewed the breakfast down. Real food would come later if the river was kind. The father tended to the river and the boy to the hearth. There was a bucket which contained the embers and coal from the fire of the day before. Sometimes they kept hot through the night and the making of a new fire was easy. In the dark of winter, though, when a quick fire was needed most, the damp and cold would often kill the coals and the boy would, with shivering hands, be forced to start a new one. The embers were dead and so he found char-cloth and a fire steel and began to strike metal on stone until the cloth and kindling caught. As he did so a spark leapt from the fire and onto the floor. He was barefoot but he had no choice to stamp on the flame lest the whole cottage burn. It was a bad omen and so he ran outside, spat through the door of the hut before running widdershins around the home to prevent more ill from entering the house. His foot hurt but that seemed to be an end to his trouble for the fire was soon burning and warmth gradually began to seep back into his bones.

He had small nets to mend and so began his work. Glad to be by the fire he lost himself in this occupation until a second dark omen interrupted the day. His father was calling for his help. He put the nets down being careful to remove them from the fireside lest a mischievous *fae* or boggart be tempted to use them to catch a flame instead of a fish. He ambled to the riverbank and saw a terrible sight.

The river was breaking. Something was shattering the ice from beneath the waters. A monster? Nan of the waters coming in rage to take his father? He would not be the first fisherman she had claimed… God save us.

'Get aways, Father!' he yelled. But his father was clearly trying to use a pathetically small net and pole to fend off the attacking creature.

'Here boy, here!' Called his father. The boy realised he wasn't trying to fight the creature off but trying to catch it. Was he mad? Doing such a thing would being doom upon himself and all the village. You did not tingle and tangle with the other folk. You paid them certain respects and minded your own business in the hope they would leave you alone. Everyone knew this. Yet, here was his father, like a foolish knight, trying to slay a dragon instead of appeasing it.

A black limb kicked out from the waters. A hoof like the devils. He had imagined the maid 'o' the weeds had fins, being a water spirit, and yet here she was, coal black and kicking in fury with satanic legs.

"Boy, here I say!' commanded his father. Then a face erupted from the water. Black again, white teeth bared and water hissing from its nostrils. The thing… the thing looked like a horse. "Here!' shouted his father, 'here!'

The boy sped to his father's aid and took hold of the pole, while his father, took the net which had caught on the pommel of the saddle. The beast was struggling. Not so much resisting the waters but trying desperately and with increasingly failing energy to swim.

'Hit her, boy!' cried his father. He was not a cruel man and could see the creature was already doomed. The boy had seen it too though usually with a sheep, or once a cow who had fallen in. They would always die, or already be dead. Once Jenny had embraced them there was no going back and yet he could not do it. The horse was struggling now. Fear seemed to have left it, and it was failing to kick. If they didn't haul her in then she would simply go in and under and, most likely be washed up somewhere down river in a week or so. 'Hit her a-sconce! The pole to her pate, boy!'

The creature looked at the boy with dark eyes. They seemed, to him full of confusion as to why it could not live anymore. He stood there frozen and wishing he could calm her thoughts. Suddenly, he found the net pressed into his hands and the weight of the current and the steed was pulling him into the river. Frantically he tried to stop himself being dragged in and began to feel the same sense of confusion and panic as the horse that was drowning in the river. The father had picked up the pole and cracked its head. The noise of the breaking skull was dreadful and the beast began to sink and the boy was nearly in the waters before the father grabbed both him and the net and pulled them back.

The net was beginning to tear, but now that the horse was no longer kicking, it was easy to lay hold of a leg. There was no hesitation now and the task was clear. They worked hard to shift the weight of the beast from water to bank. It was hard and they both, more than once, nearly found themselves in the river. When it was done they lay still next to the dead horse. There were breathing heavily; the air from their lungs being carried like smoke into the winter air. The boy looked at his father who was grinning from ear to ear.

'Yon saddle will fetch mor'n a penny,' he said with a chuckle.

The boy was confused. The saddle? Was that what all this had been about?

'Fetch me my sack. The big 'un. I've some cuttin' and then uz leave this 'ere river and gets uz to market!'

He had done as he was asked. He even cut out the creature's teeth for there was a blind woman in Marton who used bone and the like for various tools and did not mind laying on a shilling for such things. The rest of the horse would not sell and its meat was surely ruined by the river – though the cold would keep it for now – and they could see if the horse's flank or rump was worth a spit later.

'Jenny's been kind to uz,' said his father as they trudged from the bank towards the town's market. The boy was carrying the heavy sack and wasn't so sure.

'May as be, we shouldn't have taken her from the waters?' he said. He was worried that when they returned the river would have run high in its anger and washed away their home.

'May as be,' replied his father. 'But if Jenny had wanted her then Jenny would have kept her.'

The boy felt reassured by this until the knight on the horse came. His father had pressed a reassuring hand on the boy's shoulder and bid him stay where he were. Then, out of earshot, his Father had talked to the man. He seemed friendly enough but there had been many queer things had happened that day and, although the man smiled, the boy did not trust him.

A gold coin was pressed into his father's palm and they returned to the bank with the knight trotting alongside. The boy couldn't help notice that this man's saddle, though as fine as the one they had pulled from the waters, was a good deal more worn. It had seen the mark of knife, nail and cudgel. The good sir knight clearly had seen a battle or two.

He had made them fish for the fallen rider though, unless Jenny wanted him coughed up, it was a fool's errand. Nothing came of the nothing and so the father and the man talked some more. It was gentle at first and all was well. Then, it became clear that the knight wanted the boy's father to go somewhere else. His father refused. The other villagers came out to see what the nonesuch was all about but the knight paid them no mind. Another coin was offered but this time the fisherman refused it. The voices were raised. The boy's neighbours looked nervous but did not intervene. Finally, his father threw his arms in the air and then turned his back on the knight. It was a bold act and the knight did not take the gesture well. He struck the fisherman from behind and felled him to the floor. The boy felt sick. The knight flung his father on the back of his horse. Tying his hands and legs with a thin rope from a saddle back. Yes, this knight had seen battle. Now his father was like a fish himself and off to be carried who knows where.

The knight came for the boy and the boy did not run. He did not know what to do.

'Fetch me the saddle boy and your father may yet live,' spat the knight in the boy's face. His breath stank of wine and there was meat stuck fast in-between his teeth.

The boy gave him sack and saddle and watched his father be taken. He prayed to God that his father might be returned safe and then he ran. He ran hard and fast to Wickham. He had spent his life living slow on a river bank and was not used to running but he ran because he needed help. It was known that Edward of Wickham knew how to find the only one who could save his father.

He ran because the Hooded Man was who he needed.

The Sheriff was now free and both he and Robin waited for the priest to return. The pain in Robin's legs was increasing and, although he hated to admit it, he felt himself at the Sheriff's mercy. Robert de Rainault was himself uncomfortable with the notion that, were it not for the notorious wolfshead in front of him, he would have no chance of escape. Then again, perhaps this was an opportunity.

'You know', the Sheriff began, 'it's always possible for an outlaw to be pardoned.' Robin remained silent. He was listening for the priest. 'Your act of generosity, were it to be known more widely, would certainly bring you favour.'

'I want nothing from you,' said Robin, though he realised the he would welcome the Sheriff's silence. If word reached the others he had *saved* the Sheriff's life what would be said about him them. He would be at best a fool and at worst a collaborator. How could the people... how could *his* people trust him ever again?

'Well, you say that you want nothing and yet, I find, everyone always wants something. Clearly, you're not interested in money. You're perfectly capable of robbing that for yourself.' Robin, shot him a look. The Sheriff smiled. 'But there are things besides money, aren't there? Freedom for example.'

'I *am* free,' said Robin.

"'Free? Yes. Of course. Free to freeze in winter. Free to poach the king's deer and free to pay for it with your life when you are finally caught. It's a life, I suppose, but it's not a good one, is it? A man with your skills could do better.'

'As could you. You could serve the people instead of yourself.'

'Serve myself? Really? The peasants want one thing, the pope and the holy church want another and then, his Majesty, I'm sure, he'll be wanting some kind of royal due. Serve myself? I barely have time to button a tunic and you think I swan around doing only as I please.'

'Don't you?'

'Not without good men to help take the labour from me. You want the forest life? What say I give it to you?'

'I already have it,' said Robin calmly.

'You have nothing but a hiding place. Come out into the open. Serve me with bow and blade and I will make you Warden of Sherwood. Keeper of the King's Greenwood. Your ragged band of assorted assailants could be your verderers. You hold back the poachers and the bandits and, perhaps, help yourself to a little venison from time to time.' The Sheriff gave him a slow, enormous and extremely laboured wink. 'You could give yourself, and me, a quieter life.'

'And the people?'

'Are not your concern, ' said the Sheriff bluntly, 'But, if the warden of the forest were to have an issue then I am sure I would be more likely to lend my ear to that fine fellow over and above a brigand who smells like deadwood and mushrooms. You could have a real life. Help protect your people by upholding the law instead of breaking it. Be paid for your service. Why… you could even buy yourself a new hood.'

'I'd rather die.'

'Yes. Well, I am sure if you are too fool to listen, then I shall be forced to grant your request. I just wish we could have come to a more peaceful arrangement. '

'Be quiet!' whispered Robin.

'There you are you see! Too stupid to make a reasonable case like a reasonable man and so you demand silence. I think you know, red-breast, that you would make an excellent tyrant!'

'He's coming,' hissed Robin insistently. 'The priest is coming.'

Evidently the outlaw's ear were sharper than the Sheriff for he could hear nothing. Then, slowly, soft footsteps could be heard. The priest stepped forward. It was strange but each time he came from the dark he always seemed a larger man than from the time before. He was smiling again but the smile seemed a little sad. He held a makeshift noose in his hand. He looked pleasantly at Robin. 'You have recovered.'

'My legs...' protested Robin, feebly.

'I can see it in your spirit. You have recovered and now there is work to do. I am glad the cold did not take you. Where then would be the sacrifice? It is Christmas and a healthy offering must be made.' The Priest slipped the noose around Robin's neck pulling it close but not tight. 'Do not be afraid, little wolf, for I will turn you into a precious lamb'.

The priest held fast to the rope with one hand and moved to untie Robin from the pillar. That was when Robin darted forward. He was fast but not as fast as he could be. Nevertheless, the priest who had not been expecting it, stumbled and nearly let go of the noose.

Robert jumped onto the priest grabbing him by the hair. He intended to smite the cleric's head against the pillar but did not have the strength. The priest, simply stood up with the Sheriff hopelessly clinging to his massive torso.

Robin got both his hands on the tether of the noose to pull it from his captor's grasp but the Priest, apparently undisturbed by the Sheriff's pathetic efforts, simply yanked the rope hard. The noose bit hard into Robin's neck. He found his breathing tight and impossible. His hands clawed at the noose working frantically to remove it from his throat but he was already losing vision. Through a blurred lens he saw the priest drop the rope and pick up the Sheriff and dash him hard against the pillar and drop him to the floor like a stone.

They had failed.

And now they would die.

It started with an arrow.

It was shot from Nottingham castle to a plague wagon outside the walls.

Bela was a serving woman who had spent most of her recent days trying to escape the groping hands of the noble Gilbert de Grant who had recently come to the castle with a band of 'merry' knights. Well, merry was one word for it. Still, she knew her place. 'Yes m'lord.' 'No, m'lord'. Keep quiet and keep busy. She was born poor but a Friar had once helped to look after her family by providing them with gold when they were in most need. He helped them to find a better life. He had also spent time with the girl and taught her the use of herbs both culinary and medicinal in the hopes she might find her way in the world. Her skill got her into first the kitchen of the castle and then, finally, a place serving at the Sheriff's table. She never forgot his kindness and would often send him messages, in a variety of ways, to keep him aware of the castle's business.

A man had been brought to table. A man with a sack. The Sheriff had gone missing and Gisburne and the knights were preparing to ride, in fury, for an old church by the river near Marten. She would hate to be the Sheriff if these fellows were in charge of the rescue. They preened like cockerels of the morning. Armour was cleaned and swords sharpened and a fresh banner prepared for them to ride under. Gisburne was losing his mind over the fuss but, then, he had been back from the morning hunt with time to warm his toes. 'Knights', the minstrels sang, 'were valiant', but, by his blood, they were slow. It would take them an hour or more to be ready. Meanwhile, she had scribed as best she could the news of the day on a scroll from her secret stock of parchment. She was barely literate but hard study meant that, though her words were poor, the note would be understood. The parchment was fixed to arrow and the arrow fixed to bow. Then, Bela of Wickham let her message fly. Knights were slow but arrows were swift.

Tuck, from his position on the plague wagon, which no soldier dare go near, heard it land. Since Much had run foolishly into the forest the rest of them had been searching high and low. Marion sent Tuck to Nottingham in case the worst had happened. Now there was news but not, alas, of Much. The sooner Robin returned from his hunt the better. Tuck drove the Wagon back towards Sherwood stopping only to unleash a second arrow with the same note attached. The arrow travelled fast until it reached the second station. Nasir was looping the southern edge of Sherwood counterclockwise. With every loop he would check the arrow post for news. On the third loop he found Tuck's arrow. Running swiftly through the Forest he found his mark and sent another arrow to Wickham. Fina, one of the smallest girls in the village saw the arrow land and, using all her strength, plucked it from the ground and brought it to Meg. Meg, gave the girl a kiss in return for the note, and went to find her father.

But Edward was busy. He had returned from Sherwood with Meg's beloved, John Little. A fisherboy from Marten had arrived asking for Robin and so Edward had fetched John. The boy was distressed. Knights had apparently captured his father but he did not know where they were. John was explaining that Robin could do nothing for he was hunting and would not likely return for some hours. The boy was begging for them to do something. Edward was trying to calm him. There was no point running around if they did not know where the boy's father was and it was not as if they could invade Nottingham Castle.

But Meg had the arrow. Meg knew exactly where the knights could be found. They were riding towards a church…

Gisburne was glad to be riding into the day. At his command was a merry company of brutes with fine horses and even finer weapons. For too long had he been on the Sheriff's leash but now, finally, he could make his own decisions. He wouldn't have to try and lead the usual half-wit rabble plucked from the dungheaps of Nottinghamshire. In truth, they were little more than thugs and, although he attempted to train them, they were more at home swinging a fist in a tavern than a sword in battle. Now, he had trained men. Men like him.

They rode hard and fast and, by God, they needed to make up for lost time. They might have swords worth more than most of the villages around here but did that mean the idiots had to spend half a candle sharpening the damn things before every ride? He had barked orders at them and they had been cowed by his authority. Stephen of Wallingford seemed particularly intimidated by his words and seemed unable to speak; preferring to keep silent. He was a big man but he seemed as timid as a church mouse when Sir Guy took the reins! Well, they needed a leader. Perhaps, after their quest was over, they might ask him to take permanent charge of the noble brotherhood.

'Come on, dogs!' cried Sir Guy. Wallingford seemed to take this to heart and increased his speed. Perhaps, he was afraid that he might fall behind. The curse words were certainly helping to rouse knights. Why, even now the sorry looking church was on the horizon.

'What call you us?' cried Wallingford from atop his horse.

It was clear to Sir Guy that the man was readying himself for a bloody spree for already his face was flushed with rage. That was exactly what Guy wanted; for the men to be full of blood and vinegar and ready for a fight.

'I said, Mongrel, that you had better ready yourself for there's a priest in there who needs sending to heaven.'

'Mongrel?' cried Wallingford.

'Aye!' taunted Sir Guy, pleased that his approach was inspiring the men.

'Didn't your mother teach you to tame your tongue?' Shouted Wallingford, using his horse to cut in front of Sir Guy's own.

Guy was confused. What was he doing? This was slowing them down.

55

'Ho there! Look out where you ride!' Said Sir Guy, struggling to calm his steed.

'Dogs don't know how to ride horses,' sneered Wallingford, 'They only know how to bite.' And with those words and a practiced arm he hit Guy hard in the face and watched, with more than a little satisfaction, as the fool fell from his horse.

Guy found himself with a face full of snow. He dragged himself up out of the snow to see that Swynbourne had recovered his now riderless horse and had put the reins in the hands of that slug-born fisherman. The other knights had ceased their ride and were looking to Wallingford to see what he would do.

Wallingford was off his mount and coming for Gisburne. His sword wasn't drawn. Guy got to his feet. He wasn't confused anymore. He was ready and he was angry. It would be with fists then. Wallingford swung with a fast left but it came too early and Guy, who was lean and spry, easily moved out of the way. The manoeuvre put him too far to counter and so he waited for Wallingford to come to him. The armour and the snow made Stephen's approach unhelpfully sluggish and Gisburne was strong enough to put a well-placed kick in the fellows gut as he came forward. It hit, but caused no pain, serving only to slow the knight down. Guy followed up with a sharp right. Gauntlet hit helmet and both men felt a shocking reverberation as the blow hit home. A second blow followed with an uppercut to Sir Guy's chin. Sir Guy found the strike caused him to taste blood in his mouth, but, by this point, he was hitting Stephen again and again. His fist hurt and he could tell his knuckles were scraping raw inside his metal glove. It was then that Wallingford, from his bent-double position, twisted his hips sharply giving powerful momentum to a well-placed shove. Gisburne had been lured in too close and had sacrificed his balance. It was not a punch which decided the fight but a flat hand strategically pushing Sir Guy's chest causing him to end up flat on his back. The Bachelor Knights gave a cheer and, for the first time in his life, Gisburne wished that the Sheriff was here.

'I yield!' said Sir Guy, offering his humiliated hand to Wallingford and expecting to be pulled up.

Stephen of Wallingford couldn't give a fig for courtly manners. That was for the stories. Sir Guy had called him a mongrel, well then, let him see how a swine fights. He stomped hard on Guy's chest knocking all the breath from his body.

Guy fell flat. His eyes widened in shock. Surely... the fellow wouldn't actually dare to harm him?

Wallingford unsheathed his sword. He was slow and deliberate. He wanted the man to see it coming.

Sir Guy realised that this would be his end. His throat began to go dry.

'You can't kill him,' cried John Salveyn, 'He's the Sheriff's man.'

'The Sheriff isn't here.' replied Wallingford, stepping back in order to give himself a better thrust.

Gisburne thought for a moment about pleading for his life before deciding he wouldn't give the man the satisfaction. If he was to die then he would die; and he would do it spitting in the mercenary's face.

'They'll come after us. When they've found we've taken a King's man,' put in Arrington.

'Who's to tell who did it?' Said Gilbert. 'We'll dump him in the river. The fisherman too.'

At this the fisherman, who was already feeling sick to his stomach, began to lose control of himself. "Please... masters, I won't speak. No need for me to say what I seen.'

The knights ignored him. They were more concerned with the problem of Gisburne, after all no one would miss a fisherman.

'We could dump them in the forest?' suggested Arrington. 'Blame it on the outlaws.'

'Sherwood,' agreed Wallingford, and raised his sword.

'Wait!' cried Swynbourne. 'There's a boy watching!'

Stephen put his sword down and turned, with the rest of the knights, to see, in the distance a small, slender figure running from the forest towards the church. 'Put the boy in the earth!' cried Stephen, but, Salveyn had already fired his crossbow at the child.

'Ride!' said Arrington leading the charge towards the young witness. He was followed by a somewhat unsteady John de St-Calais and Gilbert de Grant. Salveyn cursed, for he had missed the boy. Still, there was time enough to change that. He re-primed his weapon and raced to catch the others.

Swynbourne shoved the fisherman into the snow and drew a long sharp knife. When it came to a close kill he always abandoned his more expensive knightly weapons for something more simple and efficient. 'I'll do mine and you do yours.' He said.

Wallingford nodded and raised his sword over Gisburne again whilst the remaining knights bachelor fired once again upon the fleeing boy.

The priest had waited a long time for this moment. He had seen too much of the sickness. He had bred too much of the sickness. Time and time again the King would say that, if the land was to be at peace, then the infidel must be destroyed. Only when Edessa was returned to Christendom would the violence be at an end. But, that had been said about Jerusalem. It was a lie. It was always a lie.

When he had returned to England things were no better. There were no infidels here and yet there seemed to be as much bloodshed as anywhere else. What was to be done? He found prayer difficult. He went through the motions but often, upon shutting his eyes, all he could see were the images of bloody deeds done long ago. He wanted it all to stop. Please God let it stop. He had put into practice all his healing arts in the hope that the land might be restored but, it seemed to him, the more he worked the more there was to do.

Even here, in the very sanctuary, he wasn't protected from those who had been infected. He had seen the man fishing in the river and had politely asked if the fellow could fish elsewhere. If the eels were all taken then he would have none to offer to the poor; besides there were plenty of other spots along the river. The man had grown abusive, calling down curses with no respect for man or God. Eventually the man left and all was well. That was until the man returned with a cudgel. He had come early and filled his trap with eels then he had lit a fire at the base of the church and waited for the priest to come out. They had exchanged words and he remembered trying to put out the fire feeling sick in his stomach. That was when the fisherman sought to smite him. He grieved, for his old life came back to him as sure as night follows day. They fought. Both of them infected with the sickness and he wept as the man fell. Much to his shame he had killed the man as easily as was the act of breaking bread. He knew he too still had the disease. He had offered, like an Isaac, the man's body in the hope he might be forgiven; placing his tithe of eels within the corpse. But the images still came to him and he realised the sacrifice had not been acceptable.

Then these notorious men had been delivered to him. The notorious hooded horror of the forest who, with his robber band, attacked merchants and nobles along with the Sheriff of Nottingham, a thug who crushed the poor under his boot. They were emblems of all that was wrong with the world. Yet it was a gift. A sign. How had they come here to his very sanctuary on this very day? It was clearly significant. The eel-man was a poor unfortunate but these others, well, they had chosen to plague the land. They were professionally violent. Surely, the gift of their deaths would be worth more? It is written that Cain, had sacrificed poorly and was forced to roam the land with the mark of murder upon his head. But, now, mercifully, he, unlike Cain, had another chance. Now he could be an Abel and do something which would delight the Lord. Perhaps this act would finally put an end to the bloodshed.

He stared at them. The Sheriff was still out cold. The outlaw was furiously trying to escape. Even now, as they looked at one another, both men realised that it was too late. He held his long knife. This was not an act of violence, he told himself, this was a sacrifice to stem the tide. Two deaths to save many. He approached the altar with a firm resolve.

Robin saw the priest approach. Despite his frantic attempts to, once again, remove his bonds this time they were not giving way. The unbound Sheriff was unconscious and unable to help. The priest came closer and Robin wished that, were his life to be sacrificed, it would actually save the people. That his death might mean something. Perhaps, afterwards, there would be another hooded man who could continue what he begun.

The fire had once again been lit and the fire crackled casting shadows on the wall. It lit the priest as he approached. It seemed to Robin that he was no healer nor no monster but just another frightened man with a knife in his hand unsure of what was to come. Then, a sharp burst of wintery air flooded the church and pushed the flames flat.

The doors of the church flung open and Much ran into the nave in terror. His eyes were wide in fear. He opened his mouth to speak and blood poured out.

'They're coming, Robin... they're coming,' He was pulling at his bloody stomach finally opening his hands to reveal a crossbow bolt. He looked in pained surprise before falling to the floor.

The priest dropped his blade in shock, looking at the injured boy. He was alarmed, not at the warning, but that a young man had just polluted the sanctuary with his blood. Sacrifice was one thing but murder... He must act. He could not make an offering under these conditions. He ran to gather cleansing cloths and water.

'Much!' Robin screamed.

'Be still, you imbecile!' twittered a bird-like voice in his ear. It was the Sheriff. He was awake and had clearly been, like a travelling player, enacting his own incapacitation. He was making swift work of untying Robin's bonds. 'Understand this, wolfshead, and understand it well. I free you and you are in my debt. You are my man, now!'

Robin, could barely take in the Sheriff's words. He was staring at his brother lying still on the stone floor. The bonds fell and the Sheriff was off the altar and had picked up the priest's abandoned knife.

59

'I am going to run, now and you… you will take care of our friend, the mad monk! This is my command!' The Sheriff said waving the knife in Robin's face. He thought about ending the outlaw at that very moment but a fight with the rogue would not be quick and the noise would soon bring the pitiless priest back. No. Leave the hood and the cowl to fight amongst themselves and give him more time to haste his heels back to the safety of the approaching knights. With them, in tow, he could return would have the pleasure of killing them both at his leisure. 'Kill the priest!' he said, spitting the words into Robin's face before running into the shadows of the church.

Robin rolled from the altar. His legs still gave him pains but there was a fury in him now that surpassed his weakness. He ran to Much's side. Was he still breathing? Was the wound deep? His hands went across the body but there was no hole only stained clothes and the stink of deer remains. Was this deer blood? Much turned his head and winked at him and Robin realised it was a knave's trick. 'I come for you, Robin,' said his brother as he slipped Robin a dagger so artfully that even Robin didn't notice until he felt the handle in his free hand.

"Lay still, 'said Robin, scanning the church for signs of danger.

The priest was nowhere to be seen and the Sheriff had also vanished. The light of the burning brazier was diminishing and the newly snow-filled sky with its ominous clouds was making the church increasingly dark. Now it was impossible to tell who was hunting who. The words of Herne echoed around his mind.

In the Season of the Christ Child the Eel and the Wolf and the Hawk did dance a furious jig; and where one finished and the other began… no man could tell. And in that dance there was a kiss and a death and a saving but who did what to whom… no man could tell.

The fisherman's boy did as he was told. The knights were in the distance and now they were riding for him. Now, they were firing at him. He was not fast but he did not need to be. It was a short distance into the forest.

Arrington was the fastest and reached the tree-line first. After this morning's misadventure he had no intention of riding into the undergrowth and so alighted from his horse. He was tying it to a tree as de Grant, Salveyn and John caught up.

'I'll not ride in there. Not after what happened to me' John de St-Calais said as he brought his steed to a halt.

'It'll slow us.' warned Gilbert, getting of his mount.

'Slow won't matter if you shoot straight. Nothing faster than a crossbow,' responded Arrington who was already moving into the dark of the forest.

The three knights followed. They could see Arrington moving forward. There was a clear path and the boy had not had the sense to avoid it.

'I see him!' cried John De St-Calais pointing down the track.

Arrington braced himself. He had the child in his sights.

'Please!' cried the boy who had turned to face his pursuers.

'Be still!' commanded Arrington. His bolts were made by a man named Rivers in London. They were extremely well crafted and expensive and he did not want to use any more than he needed on this mewling infant. That would be a waste.

The boy suddenly sprang away. Arrington stopped himself from firing at the last minute. He cursed but, at least, he hadn't put a bolt into a tree. The knights followed. Although the boy was gone from sight they were easily gaining on him now. He could only hide for so long. They had moved into a more spacious area where the trees and bushes were more evenly spaced. The knights scanned the territory, watching for movement. All was quiet.

'Leave the boy alone,' she said.

The knights turned in surprise. The red-haired woman had appeared from nowhere. She was unarmed.

'Why here's a pretty present!' cried Gilbert de Grant, lowering his crossbow, 'And where did you spring from, m'lady?'

Arrington had no time for nonsense. 'Where's the boy?'

'Safe' said Marion of Leaford.

'Not from us, he's not.' Said John de St-Calais.

'Better for you that you give us the boy,' said Arrington.

'Better for you that you leave him be,' replied Marion.

Salveyn was amazed that a woman could be so bold. He handed his crossbow to Gilbert, smiled, and began to approach her with his hands outstretched. 'Give us the boy and no harm shall come to you.'

'Don't make promises we shan't keep,' said Gilbert, who had become quite certain that the red-haired woman would make a truly entertaining captive.

'The boy!' demanded Arrington.

'I warned you,' said Marion firmly. Why would fools never listen?

'We'll find him anyway.' Said Arrington. 'Take her!'

Salveyn pounced as Marion calmly stepped back. He screamed in pain as an arrow from John's bow pierced his hand.

'To arms!' cried Gilbert, dropping Salveyn's weapon and running for cover. Arrington had already found protection behind a big beech tree. More arrows followed and it was unclear from which direction they were coming.

John de St-Calais could see the boy running north. He took up the pursuit. He risked an arrow in his back but, a moving target was surely harder to hit. Besides his armour was of good quality and it would be a rare shot that would bring him down. If he could just get the boy then, perhaps, he could trade his life for a way out of this mess.

Salveyn was in retreat. His crossbow lay forgotten on the dank earth. He was abandoning the trees. If only he could to get back to his horse. He could hear someone screaming in pain and it took him a moment to realise that the voice was his own. He stumbled out of the forest and saw his horse. A friar was there along with a plague wagon. Medicine was at hand. He was saved.

'Help me, Brother!' cried Salveyn as he ran towards the cleric.

'Indeed, I shall,' said Tuck, putting the man to sleep with a sharp dose of his quarterstaff.

The fisherman was weeping in the snow. The knight he had hoped would buy his saddle was now preparing to take his life. It would be a bloody day for all for even as he, a low-born man, was preparing to face death so too was the noble Sir Guy of Gisburne.

'Keep still!' barked Swynbourne, 'else I make a mess of it and that will go worse for you.'

The fisherman was making a pathetic crawl on his belly through the snow; a last attempt to escape. Piers sighed and put his knife away. Pulling this fool up would take two hands.

Stephen of Wallingford looked down at Gisburne. His sword was poised for the kill. Gisburne looked up at Wallingford. Why wouldn't the wretch just get it done? But Wallingford was staggering back now. Fumbling with his sword – desperately trying to put it back in his scabbard.

'Piers!' he cried.

Swynbourne had pulled the fisherman up onto his knees. He held the man's hair even as he, once again, drew the knife from his belt.

'Swynbourne!' cried Stephen.

Piers heard the cry. What was it now? He looked away only to see Wallingford scrambling for his horse. He followed the knight's gaze and saw a horseman almost upon them. The business must be done quick, then. He turned back to finish the fisherman but instead found himself confronted by another horseman who, without hesitation, put a sword through Swynbourne's visor. The knight staggered backward before careering forward and finally falling dead on the snow.

The fisherman looked at the ferocious looking man on the horse. He began to tremble.

'Don't fear, fishmaster,' said Will Scarlet as he dismounted. 'We got your boy and he's safe.'

'What about the other one?' asked the Fisherman. 'Sir Guy?'

Scarlet realised who the other man on the ground was. He spun around only to find that Gisburne was gone.

Wallingford meanwhile had ridden a short circuit to give himself some distance from the approaching rider. He knew a knight on the ground would never beat a man on horse and so, to his indignation, he had been forced to abandon the pleasure of taking revenge. He had moved quickly and managed to remount and ride out with ease. Nevertheless the rider was now close and charging with some skill. Wallingford turned his horse around and with a strong sword arm rode to meet this new enemy.

Scarlet saw the riders clash. His friend, Nasir, was fast but the knight was the bigger man and he knew that each parry would take a troubling toll on the Saracen. He took up his bow and hastily fired at the knight. It was a poor shot but enough to distract Wallingford who then took a blow from Nasir. Wallingford's armour withstood the strike and he retaliated by striking, not his opponent, but Nasir's horse who instantly began to bolt. Scarlet watched as the horse ran in the opposite direction with his friend doing all he could do stay on the beast's back. One bad turn surely deserved another and so he notched another arrow and shot the knight's horse. The beast was trained and used to the cruelties of war. The arrow hit its unprotected flank. It skittered but it did not break from obeying its master. Wallingford calmed his horse and began to ride for the outlaw. There wasn't time for another arrow or for him to remount his horse and so Scarlet drew his sword. He was on the ground and about to be charged by a heavily armoured knight. This wasn't good. He thought back to his time as a soldier in France. A situation like this never ended well.

'You best run now, master,' he called over to the fisherman. 'Get yourself home. Don't fear. My friends will bring your boy back to you.'

The fisherman hesitated.

'Run!' screamed Will. And the fisherman ran, not once looking back, for he did not want to witness the death of the man who had saved him.

Much had run to the church for aid. What he had seen, when he had first crept into the Sanctuary, was a gigantic priest threatening Robin and the Sheriff. He knew he could not fight the man and there was no time to run back to the secret caves for the others. As he fretted over what to do his hands had gone to his pouch to take some nourishment from the portion of deer he had placed there. What he found was the crossbow bolt and a plan.

He had run from the church and back to the deer carcass. He did not know why but in his foolishness he brought the corpse to the church when he could more easily have applied its blood to himself back in the forest. He really was a dolt. This dolt however, would, he determined, still save his step-brother's life. He applied the deer's blood to his clothes. He was even able to dig into its deeper parts where the blood was still liquid and take a mouthful. He had seen Scarlet do it once, as a jest, causing Much a great deal of tears. Now he would use the jape towards a more serious purpose.

And it had worked. The priest was gone and Robin was free and staring gratefully at him as he lay on the floor of the church. But something was wrong. Robin was frozen. It was as though he could not move. All was deathly quiet again. The silence was unnerving. It could be them next.

'We needs to go!' said Much. Robin nodded and yet he did not stir. 'What's wrong?'

'I can't leave,' said Robin.

'You're not going back for him, are you? Not for the Sheriff?' cried Much in disbelief.

"Him? No. The priest took my sword. He has Albion.'

'But you can't stay and fight. You're wounded.' Much was looking in distress at Robin's real wounds which were beginning to bleed again. 'We can come back.'

'Lay still,' said Robin firmly. 'Keep sharp'

Much nodded but Robin could tell the boy was fearful. Robin moved quietly back into the sanctuary. It was darker now than it had ever been. The fire was still burning but it was low and the black smoke of its dying coals found its way into Robin's lungs causing him to gag. Albion had been entrusted to him and he could not leave it behind. He could not say how but, it seemed to him, that he knew where the sword was. That in some strange way the weapon was calling to him. He found himself moving back towards the altar. As he drew nearer he could see no sign of the sword but he could see the Sheriff, bloodied from the trials of the day, standing against the wall with Albion in his hand.

The Sheriff looked up to see Robin coming.

'Did you lose something?' said the Sheriff. 'Other than the boy, of course.'

'I thought you were running,' said Robin, trying to take his eyes from looking at the precious sword. He did not what the Sheriff to know how important it was.

'I was. Then I found this. And I thought how much future grief I might be spared if I simply skewered you with it.'

The Sheriff lunged at Robin moving surprisingly fast. Robin sprung backwards giving him some distance. Much remained still, playing out his role as a dead man. The Sheriff paid him no heed. *Never reveal what need not be revealed.* Robin palmed Much's knife hoping to fool his attacker into believing he had the advantage. The Sheriff moved overconfidently, using wide swings trying to force his prey into a corner. The sword, was awkward in the Sheriff's hands and Robin could not tell whether it was simply too large for him to wield or that the sword itself was somehow resisting its new master.

He sidestepped and so did the Sheriff. Another lunge and a double back, a swipe and a spin. Robin's legs continually buckled and it took all he had to push through the pain and force them to obey. It was a grotesque and awkward dance. Robin, continued to keep his knife hidden and continued to back into a corner pulling the Sheriff towards Much. Seeing Robin now backed into the cold stone wall the Sheriff rushed forward with fast and furious jabs.

'Now, Much!' yelled Robin, and Much sprang from his position grabbing the Sheriff's leg causing him to stumble. Robin sprang forward and gripped the Sheriff's sword hand hard whilst revealing his own blade. For the second time that day his ears drummed as the blood pounded. His heart a drum of war… urging him on… urging him to claim the Sheriff's life.

'No!' came a plaintiff cry. Not from the Sheriff but from the priest who had returned with cloths and water at the other end of the church. The horror in his scarred face was amplified by the dancing flames of the nearby brazier as if the priest was a denizen of hell itself. He did the only thing he could to prevent him witnessing the desecration. He put out the only remaining light by pouring the cleansing water onto the fire. The church was plunged into real darkness with only the shine of winter coming through the main doors.

Robin lost his bearing and then his grip as the Sheriff rolled to the floor. De Rainault knew he could not compete with the strength of the outlaw but his smaller size and speed made him a difficult target. Robin spun around in the dark, the knife in his hand trying to locate his enemy. He was resisting the urge to simply kill. Taking him back to Sherwood could give them some real bargaining power but it was hard to see and as he moved through the church he could not find the devil anywhere.

Suddenly he felt a presence to his left. Quickly, he inverted the knife in his right hand ready to stun his target before realising, just in time, it was Much.

'Robin! Come on!' the boy said.

It made no sense for them to continue to blunder about in darkness and so they ran for the doors. Robin was ready for either Sheriff or priest to pounce but, as they swiftly made their exit, none came and so they stumbled free.

Marion's plan had almost worked. She and John would tire the heavily armoured men by running lightly and swift deeper into Sherwood. The knights would exhaust themselves in their pursuit and then become easier to deal with. Should they give up the chase then the outlaws would simply turn around, and pursue them with warning arrows, forcing them to either take up the chase again or surrender their arms.

That part, at least, was working. Gilbert de Grant and Nicholas Arrington were moving more slowly and cautiously. The larger knight had used all his bolts and had slung his crossbow on his back. The wilier Arrington was casting his sharp eyes around hoping for a clear shot. What Marion, had not planned for was the fisherboy's panic. Instead of heading west he had ran north and was being pursued by another knight. She only hoped Herne would protect him.

A bolt whistled past her.

'Watch out, Marion!' hissed John from behind a nearby oak. She hadn't been paying attention, too busy thinking about the boy.

'Now?' she asked.

'Now' agreed John. Whilst Arrington was skillfully reloading his crossbow, no easy task in these conditions, John let another warning arrow fly and Marion ran to the next tree.

John Little hadn't intended to kill Gilbert de Grant but a sudden gust of wind took his arrow and delivered it neatly under the knight's casque and through the man's throat. He lifted his arms instinctively trying to remove the offending missile but his instincts lasted only as long as his remaining breath and he soon dropped to the floor like a stone down a well.

Arrington saw him fall and became enraged. He let his crossbow fall, drew his sword and charged at John with neither wit nor wisdom.

John met him with quarterstaff in hand. It was the most foolish battle of the day. A small exhausted knight, slowed by armour, taking on the biggest man in Sherwood who was fighting on home territory. Arrington charged and John simply waited for him to come before extended his staff and hitting the man squarely in the chest. Arrington flew backwards landing on his rump like a small child who was being schooled by a teacher.

Crack.

The staff smashed down in Arrington's helmet. John only wanted to knock the man out but he was, however, a little too earnest and Arrington was killed instantly.

Marion realising that John was not following returned to the scene with bow in hand. She saw John looking a little shame-faced as he stood, like a mountain, above the two fallen knights.

'We didn't need to kill them,' she said.

'I'm sorry.' John replied, and, for a while, there was nothing but silence.

Will Scarlet had often wished he were dead. He had wished it many times when his wife had been taken. As the Knight rode towards him in all his fury and finery it made him think that of all the ways to go it would not be under a Norman blade. No.

Wallingford charged and Will had forgotten just how fast and terrifying a warhorse can be when it runs directly at you. The dread of it did not make you flee but, instead, it froze you to the spot. It was a kind of fearful sorcery that charmed your heels and stuck them to the floor. Still, he was not one of those that paid much attention to fear or magic and so he waited as long as he dared before jumping left and swiping at the horse.

He jumped too soon and too far. Fear had got the better of him and he was nowhere near close enough to hit his mark. He cursed himself for his cowardice and waited for another chance. There was no other strategy and both men knew it. Notch an arrow and, before he had time to let it fly, he would be run down. Run for the trees and, before he reached the half way mark, he would be run down. Stand in the way and wait long enough before jumping aside and he might, just might, be able to unseat the knight.

Another charge came. Wallingford wasn't even bothering to use his sword. That would mean slowing his horse and, in these circumstances, his horse combined with its speed was far deadlier than any blade.

The horse came, faster this time and Will waited too long. He jumped aside but the force of the passing steed knocked him off balance. He had dropped his sword and quickly got onto his feet. The horse was already coming for him a second time but then, so was another.

Gisburne!

Wallingford saw the second rider but too late. He pulled up from his charge at Will and had just enough time to draw his blade to meet Sir Guy's furious attack.

Scarlet could barely believe it. They were fighting each other. He wanted to put an arrow in both of them but there, in the distance, he could see two figures stumbling out of a nearby church and third man, an archer, about to shoot them both. He grabbed bow and sword and moved to remount; but not before he loosed an arrow. He shot at the two knights not caring which of the men it struck and then rode towards the church.

Gisburne was shocked to see Wallingford fall from his horse. An arrow had unseated him. Sir Guy whirled his own horse around to see if he would be next target but found, surprisingly, the bowman was riding away.

Wallingford was struggling to stand. He was surprised. He always thought his final battle would be longer than this. Gisburne slowed his horse, dismounted and drew his sword. He could see the knight was already too weak to fight. It was then he had a merry little thought.

'If you can't join them – beat them!' he said to Stephen of Wallingford.

Stephen of Wallingford, however, did not respond for he was already dead and, not for the first time that day, Sir Guy of Gisburne was bitterly disappointed.

Nasir finally calmed his horse. The wretched beast had run north and, just when he thought he had control of it, something had scared the accursed creature into running into the forest. He had just got it back to the tree-line and had dismounted. He wanted to check that the creature wasn't injured. Then from the corner of his eye he fancied he felt a man behind them. It was a feeling that made the hairs on the back of his neck stand on end. He spun around with sword in hand but saw only a deer or, something akin to one, running away into the forest. How foolish he was. His momentary panic, however, had further rattled the nerves of his own horse which then disappeared into the trees.

He had no choice but to find the beast and so ran in after it. It wasn't hard to track, but somehow, after a point he found only deer tracks. Was he imagining it? A horse could not simply disappear.

There was something odd about the hunt. He would occasionally feel the presence of the deer; although one was nowhere to be seen. Without tracks he was running blind; that is until he heard movement in a clearing ahead. Finally. He moved swiftly and quietly so as not to disturb the terrified creature only to find something else.

A boy on the ground and one of the knights with a sword in his hand.

The head of John de St-Calais was complaining again. After the earlier incident with the tree branch it had not stopped thumping. His ears were having trouble discerning sounds and it sounded, in his mind, like they were filled with water. It was a bad day. Wallingford had been forced to kill Gisburne and the only witness was the boy that now lay in front of him. This was not a thing he took pleasure in. It was not something he wanted to do but, there again, he had done such things before and needs must.

He swung his sword and was surprised to find himself hallucinating. His broken mind imagined that he was back in the Holy Land for, there in front of him, blocking his blow was a Saracen. He lowered his sword and shut his eyes before opening them again; hoping that this visitation would go away.

The Saracen remained.

John de St-Calais opened his mouth in the hopes that by asking a question all would become clear. Instead, it all went dark; for Nasir Malik Kemal Inal Ibrahim Shams ad-Dualla Wattab ibn Mahmud killed the man where he stood.

Outside was brighter. An early moon competed with the late sun as both reflected their cold light on snow and ice; making the world seem like it was day and night at the same time. But there was a sound. An awful sound. The sound of blades being struck. In the far distance Robin could see two knights on horseback exchanging blows.

Then came the sound of other hooves coming nearer. Surely the sound of the Knights Bachelor returning to the church, realising they had been tricked and relishing the prospect of wreaking their revenge?

Robin saw the cracked ice where he and the Sheriff had fallen. He was looking for hope. He had thrown his bow and arrows aside when he had made that near fatal leap. If only he could find them now.

And there they were. Next to the body of that fateful deer which, somehow, mysteriously lay bloody on the snow before him a mile from where it was shot.

The only problem was that he was too late. Standing near the carcass was a small man with an arrow notched on a tense and quivering bowstring. He looked a lot, in the dark of the day moon's shadow, like an outlaw. The Sheriff of Nottingham gave no word of warning, nor made no jest. He simply fired.

Robin did not move. There was no time. He knew the Sheriff had a clear shot and knew that, even as he thought it, the arrow would hit home.

And it did. Directly in the heart. Tearing muscle and ripping vein and artery so well it would be forever beyond the skill of any healer.

The priest dropped to his knees. He had followed them out of the church. Broadsword in hand – a relic from his past.

Robin turned round and saw the priest on his knees in the snow, as if penitent, with an arrow firmly in his chest having pierced the inverted mail. His mouth was open in a silent scream. A mixture of sorrow and pity were in the priest's eyes; the last emotions felt before he fell, face-first, into the snow. His black teeth finally buried in the white of winter.

Robin and Much were astonished at the grace of the Sheriff. It never occurred to Robin that the Sheriff might have the capacity to be a hero. Much smiled at him. The Sheriff appeared to be in shock.

For a moment no-one could speak.

'You've saved us both' said Robin, finally finding his words.

The Sheriff looked at the outlaw with incredulity. 'I wasn't aiming for him, you dolt. Just because some cracked crusader tried to kill us both you think we're suddenly all in it together?' The Sheriff had notched a second arrow to the bow. He smiled. This time he would not miss. 'Nothing is forgotten, wolfshead.'

The arrow was released but, this time, Robin was ready and the Sheriff was truly a terrible shot. It went wide of the mark. Robin and Much ran forward and knocked the Sheriff to the ground.

Robin was soon stood holding Albion to the Sheriff's throat. Robert de Rainault glared back at him in defiance.

'Kill me and the King will send an army,' said the Sheriff, 'and he'll tax your people to pay for it!'

Oh, how he wanted to do it. To kill the High Sheriff of Nottingham – plague of the people. What was wrong with him? Robin pondered on the priest's words. Was he himself possessed of a violent sickness? And what blood would be shed in repayment for the murder of the King's Sheriff. How many ordinary people would be imprisoned and killed as a consequence for taking the life of this one particular weasel? But Robin needed no argument. He had already made up his mind. 'I don't kill the weak. I protect them.' He said and took his blade from the Sheriff's throat.

'We goin' to take him to the others, Robin?' asked Much.

Robin shook his head. There wasn't time and he could hear the approaching horse which now sounded as if it were pulling a wagon.

'Nothing is forgotten, as you say.' Robin said, 'Remember this.'

Robin hefted the heavy corpse of the bloody deer over the prostrate official. A present of sorts.

'The Keeper of the King's Deer,' Robin said.

'Feast you well,' said Much, although he wished, in his heart, they were taking the meat back to Sherwood.

The Sheriff was pinned down and too exhausted to move the stinking creature. God's blood he would make the outlaws pay for this indignity.

The approaching horse turned out to be Tuck in his wagon. The Friar was wise enough not to try and cross the ice. Instead, Much and Robin precariously found their way back across and into the transport. Will arrived at the same time and they were surprised to find a knight bound and gagged in the bed of the vehicle.

'What are we doing with this one?' asked Will.

'Ransom. There's a fisherman what's owed money for a saddle. He'll have to make do with what this rascal's family will pay,' said Tuck with a wink as they rode back to Sherwood.

'What about the rest of them?' asked Robin.

'Marion will explain. Let's just say this one got the best of it.'

This was from John who was sitting next to Tuck. Despite her scolding he was in a better mood. They had stripped the men of their very expensive weapons and armour for which he knew he could get a good price. In fact, he had this little treasure trove with him right now for he was a man. A man with a sack!

Robin gratefully shut his eyes and finally slept a true sleep. They rode slowly off back to Wickham leaving only a faint trail behind them. But that trail soon would disappear for it had already begun to snow heavily again.

Gisburne, when he finally arrived at the church, did not see their tracks for the dark had come quick. He did find a dead priest, though, and what appeared to be a feckless poacher stuck under the body of a deer. Curious, he moved the animal's corpse and was surprised to find what he had been looking for all along. He helped his master to stand.

No words were said.

More snow began to fall and so, to the Sheriff's chagrin, they were forced to retire to the only shelter available. They were cold and hungry and it was now too dangerous to travel. This really was the end to the worst of all possible days, reflected Robert, that he the High Sheriff of Nottingham and the noble Sir Guy of Gisburne were now forced to hide pathetically inside a church.

Hide as if they were low-born fugitives seeking… Sanctuary.

Richard Carpenter's

ROBIN OF SHERWOOD

THE POWER OF THREE

Jennifer Ash

You may also enjoy...

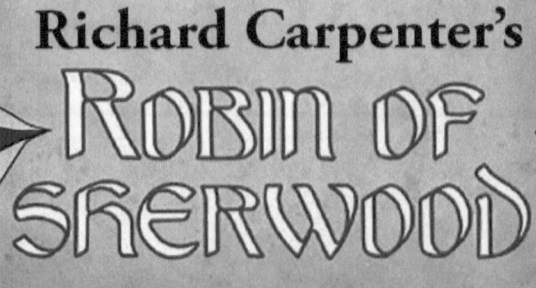

Richard Carpenter's

ROBIN OF SHERWOOD

THE MEETING PLACE

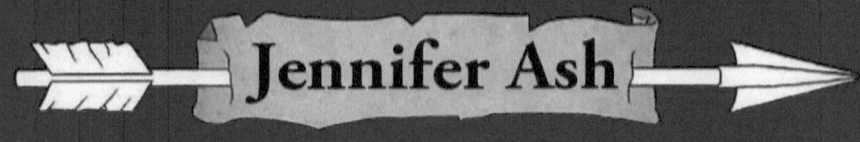

Jennifer Ash